AT LARGE

Based on the stories and characters of

BANCKS

Written and illustrated by

JAMES KEMSLEY

ANGUS
& ROBERTSON
PUBLISHERS

This book is dedicated to:

Mr Bancks,
Mr Vivian,
Mr Piper,

And their wives,
and my wife
Helen
"Because only they know"

Thanks, Peter, Bev, Lats, Sheena and Pezzie

Contents

Chapter 1
The Prisoner

"**B**OY, what a home," mumbled Ginger as he reluctantly headed towards the tool shed in the corner of the back yard. "Gee whiz, what *is* a feller around this place? An awful criminal or something? Sending him out into the blazing heat that'll probably give him sunstroke and burnt lips for life."

Ginger looked discreetly back through the kitchen door, only to see that his mother was apparently ignoring his performance. The situation called for drastic action. After all, why should a feller, or anyone for that matter, have to spend a top sunny afternoon cleaning up a yard when there were a zillion better things he could be doing instead?

He'd faint! That's what he'd do, faint. Drop down, plomp! Pass out right under the kitchen window, right under his mother's nose. She'd have to change her mind then.

First he'd have to get her attention, otherwise he'd be

lying there until dinner, as he had done last time. Not only that, but he had ended up being bitten on the bottom by an aggressive bull ant that saw him, not as a case for sympathy, but as a giant, red-headed, freckled road-block.

Ginger had learnt two important lessons that day. One, make sure you know where you are when you faint. Two, it's almost impossible to pretend you've passed out when you've been bitten on the behind by a bull ant.

He now coughed loudly. "If you come out into the yard," he raised his voice, "and y' see a feller with peeled back skin and his cheeks sunk and his eyeballs shrunk back into his head, with a terrible fever," his voice spluttered, his knees began to shake, "check him out," he gave a final cough, "he'll probably be me."

And with that, plomp! He dropped to the ground.

Ginger's two pets, Tony, his monkey, and Mike, his pup, who had been following their disgruntled master at a sympathetic but safe distance, jumped back puzzled at what had just happened. They looked at each other quizzically, then at Ginger lying like Ayers Rock in front of them, then up to the kitchen window where Mrs Meggs continued humming to herself and tidying up the lunchtime dishes.

"Oh, Ginger," she called nonchalantly, "whilst you're doing the yard, will you spray some insecticide down that old bull ant nest. I've noticed that the little blighters are back again."

Ginger's eyes popped open. The memory of that stinging hot sensation came back to him immediately.

"GEE WHIZ –
WHAT IS A FELLER AROUND THIS
PLACE ?"

"...THE LITTLE BLIGHTERS ARE BACK AGAIN."

"Surely Mum's bluffing," he thought. "But what if she's not? What if she's fair dinkum and the bull ants have come back? What if. . .what if. . .?"

The risk wasn't worth taking. He jumped up and surveyed the surrounds for his miniature foe. "Nothing! Tch!" Ginger kicked himself in the ankle. "Ow! Sucked in again," he mumbled.

He slowly set off towards the tool shed once again.

"Just my luck." He turned to Tony, hoping for some sort of simian support. "All the mums in the world, and I crack it for a smart one. It's a ripoff if you ask me; a pure one hundred per cent ripoff."

Tony blinked twice then did an enormous back flip. Ginger was sure this meant that Tony, at least, sympathised with his plight.

"It's always the same," Ginger said wistfully. "The mother being funny with the son. Always the smart answer. A feller could be dying of a terrible disease and the mother would be busy getting off some smart remark."

The back wire door slammed!

Ginger quickened his steps, not daring to look behind.

He reached the tool shed, grabbed the rake and a large green plastic bag and quickly set about filling it with the leaves and papers that were scattered about the yard.

Mrs Meggs walked up to her son. Ginger waited as her footsteps approached. Had he gone too far? Been too cheeky?

"Don't forget to sweep the path when you've finished," she said. "Use the large straw broom behind the kitchen door."

Ginger turned slowly. His mother had on her best hat and was carrying his young brother Dudley. The relief showed in his freckled face.

"Aw, Mum," pleaded Ginger desperately, "can't a feller go swimmin' at the pool? When a guy gets to a certain age, y' reckon he's got *some* rights."

"And he'll have some 'lefts' too if he isn't careful and doesn't do what he's told," retorted Mrs Meggs. "Dudley and I are going over to Mrs Perry's for afternoon tea. Remember what I said about the large straw broom behind the kitchen door."

Ginger watched silently as his mother and his brother

disappeared down the back lane and then on to the main street.

The main street! His domain, his kingdom! Except when Tiger Kelly, El Supremo bully, was about, that is.

The thought of what he might be doing was enough to make a feller depressed. If only his dad had listened to him and cemented in the back yard, as Paulo's dad had done, there would be no leaves, or grass, or anything to worry about. Then a feller could be swimming, or at the movies, or anywhere.

Ginger turned and slowly scanned the yard. It looked enormous. The size of the cricket ground at least.

"It'll take forever to clean it up," he sighed. "A feller's a prisoner, a prisoner in his own house." Again he looked to Tony and Mike for support.

Then, with all the force he could muster, Ginger kicked an empty aluminium drink can that was near his foot. It narrowly missed Tony's left ear and went sailing over the fence into the Mullinses' yard.

"Oh no!" he said. The blood drained from his sunburnt cheeks, even his freckles went pale.

Ginger silently crept towards the fence and carefully peered over the palings. There was no sign of Mr Mullins.

"Phew!"

"Psst! Hey, Ginger," a voice called to him from a knot-hole in the fence.

A familiar checkered cap, followed by a broadly smiling face, popped up from behind the back gate. It was Bennie Hooper, not only Ginger's best friend, classmate and loyal companion, but just about the

10

"PSST! HEY, GINGER!"

greatest wicket-keeper that a top fast bowler, like Ginger
Meggs, could have keeping dustbin for him.

"Caught Hooper, bowled Meggs" was a legendary
catchcry down in Gawler's Paddock. To date they had
virtually single-handedly won four hundred and twenty-
seven test matches against all comers, under all
conditions.

"Coming down to the pool this arvo, Ginge?" asked
Bennie as he slid down the paling next to his mate.

"No way, Bennie," said Ginger, downcast. "No funds.
If y' could go to England and back for fifty cents, I
haven't got enough to get out-of-sight. You're looking at
the original 'No Money Meggs'."

"We could go down to Gawler's Paddock for a bit of a
hit," said Bennie enthusiastically. "That doesn't cost

anything. We could get Ocker Stevens, Chubbie, Pez and a couple of other kids too, I reckon; and there's Mike and Tony, they can field."

Ginger sighed and shook his head. "Can't," he said. "I'd love to have a hit. I'd give my right arm to have a hit! But I've gotta clean up the yard — and just have an optic at it."

"Wow, what a tough break," said Bennie. "If I give y' a hand, we'll have it done in half the time."

"And it will still take forever," moaned Ginger. "It's typical Meggs luck. I reckon if I were to toss up a dollar, it'd come down five cents."

There was little that Bennie could say.

"Hang on," shouted Ginger suddenly. He pointed to something at the opposite end of the yard. "Take a look at that, will y'!"

A straw hat was slowly making its way along the other side of the Meggses' fence in the direction of the back lane.

Bennie did not really know what Ginger was on about and was somewhat shaken by the sudden eruption of energy.

"If I'm not mistaken," cried Ginger, with un-concealed joy, "that hat is connected to the head of none other than Cuthbert Fitzcloon, who, as it so happens, owes me a favour or two. And today, although old Cuthie doesn't know it yet, is the day I collect."

Ginger raced to the back gate and flung it open just in time to bounce in front of a startled Cuthbert.

"Good day, Cuthie, old mate. And what might you be

12

doing down this way?" asked Ginger, extra politely.

"Taking my lunchtime walk," answered Cuthbert, nervously. "It aids the digestive process. I always take a walk after lunch," he added.

"But never down this way before," countered Ginger.

There was an anguished silence. By this time Bennie, along with Tony and Mike, had arrived at the back gate. Cuthbert suddenly found himself in the centre of a discomforting circle. He tried to speak, but, much to his dismay, found that he could only grin and gulp.

Ginger remained silent, giving Cuthbert the famous Meggs "say something, turkey" grin. A grin that, to Cuthbert, looked for all the world like another he'd once seen at the zoo, whilst staring down into the alligator pit.

Finally, a word slipped out and broke the deafening silence. "A change," squeaked Cuthbert, "just for a change, Ginger."

"Not just a change," said Ginger, throwing his arm around Cuthbert's shoulder and leading him into the Meggses' back yard.

"No, not just a change," continued Ginger in a half whisper, "but fate!"

"Fate?" Cuthbert squeaked again.

"Yes fate," Ginger responded quickly. "You see, I seem to remember a recent occasion, in the not too distant past, when a certain Master C. Fitzcloon Esquire promised myself that he would do 'anything', yeah 'anything' . . ."

Ginger's tone changed. His brow blackened. His eyes opened wide as he stared deep into Cuthbert's eyes ". . . if

" NO, NOT JUST A CHANGE ...FATE."

I were to forgive him and not drop him like a cold lamb chop, for certain rude and ungentlemanly remarks he'd made concerning Minnie Peters!" he said menacingly.

Cuthbert dropped his eyes, half in fear, half in shame. "I sort of remember promising, Ginger," he said; the words stuck in his throat, "er, er . . ."

"Good," said Ginger, his mood once again cheery.

Cuthbert breathed a sigh of relief.

Even Bennie was somewhat glad the inquisition had come to an end.

Ginger walked Cuthbert further into the yard. "You see, I've decided what that 'anything' can be," he said.

Cuthbert tried to speak but Ginger continued before he was able to find the right words. "You can start by cleaning up this yard. Today, this afternoon, *now,* that is," he said.

"Er . . ." Cuthbert moaned.

"That is, unless you want the hospital to have a new customer and old Mr Flogswell to have one less kid in his class."

"Of course, Ginger. Whatever you say, Ginger. Anything. Anything!" spluttered Cuthbert, trying to hide his reluctance behind a beautiful but obviously forced smile.

Ginger grinned from ear to ear. "Good stuff!" he said. "C'mon, Bennie, seein' how Cuthbert here has volunteered to clean up my yard, I reckon it's about time you and me, and the fellers, checked out the happenings up the main street and down at Gawler's Paddock."

Ginger pulled the gate shut and he and Bennie set off

down the lane with Mike and Tony following at their heels. Ginger remembered his mother's parting words.

"Another thing, Cuthie," he called out, "don't forget to sweep up when you've finished. Use the big straw broom behind the kitchen door."

"Right, Ginge!" said Cuthbert, as he set about his awesome task.

"It shows how smart a feller can be if you can get other guys to work for you, especially if they don't want to!" confided Ginger to Bennie. "That's the secret of life, I reckon."

"Reckon," agreed Bennie, as they turned into the main street.

Chapter 2
Some Joke

"**D**O you think Cuthbert will clean up your yard, Ginger?" asked Bennie.

"Too right, he will."

"Poor old Cuthbert, he'll probably be there most of the arvo," said Bennie sympathetically.

"But he deserves it," said Ginger quickly. "After all the rotten things he said about Min, I reckon I'm doing him a favour letting him clean up the yard instead of knocking his ears off for him."

"No one can say you're not fair, Ginger," said Bennie with conviction.

"It's diplomacy," said Ginger.

Halfway down the main street Ginger and Bennie stopped at their favourite watering hole, Joe's milk bar, *the* place to see and be seen. It was run by a large jovial Italian named Franco Da Fienze. He'd kept the name, "Joe's", from the previous owner, for the sake of convenience, so all the kids called him "Joe", also for convenience.

Joe's large, thick, black handlebar moustache was his trademark, along with his unequalled talent for making the world's best strawberry sundaes and hamburgers "with the lot".

Ginger and Bennie pressed their faces against the milk bar window to ogle Joe, hard at work on one of the ice-cream masterpieces for which he was famous.

"Will ya look at that!" said Bennie.

"What I wouldn't give for one of those," said Ginger, his nose as hard against the glass as it could possibly be. "Just look at the size of that strawberry sitting on all that ice-cream."

Bennie's mouth was watering. So were Tony's and Mike's. Both were familiar with Joe's masterly creations.

Bennie smacked his lips. "It's fantabulous," he said, "nothing short of fantabulous."

"Aw, it's no use looking," said Ginger discouragingly. "Joe's given up giving credit. He reckons from now on it's cash money or nothing."

"That's because Tiger Kelly put two hamburgers 'with the lot', a super sundae supreme and a large orange juice on a Bankcard he found," said Bennie cynically. "He might even have got away with it if he hadn't signed it Vera La Moss."

Ginger groaned knowingly. "It's crook fellers like that, that ruin it for honest fellers like us," he said.

"No Money Meggs" echoed in Ginger's head. It was really depressing. He no longer felt like a hit down at Gawler's Paddock. Anyway, knowing his luck he'd probably be on 365 not out and lose the ball or

"WILL YA LOOK AT THAT!"

something. Worse still, he'd have to stop playing just to race home in time to get back before his mother, in case she discovered Cuthbert cleaning up the yard.

"Hey, Meggsie, have y' seen it?" a voice called out to them from the other side of the road, where a small crowd had gathered. The voice belonged to Paul Aloysius Michael Van der Chubbah, widely known to all and sundry as "Chubb", Meggsie's second-best friend and opening wicket partner.

"Seen what?" shouted Ginger, wondering what all the fuss was about.

"The parade! The poster about the parade."

"What parade?"

"The Australia Day parade, with the Prime Minister and everything." Chubb was breathless. He was becoming more excited each time he spoke.

"Y' joking!" chorused Ginger and Bennie. "The Prime Minister! Dead set! Y' gotta be joking! He's coming here?"

By now Ginger, Bennie, Tony and Mike, the latter having even been distracted from checking out his favourite parking meter, had crossed the street and joined the small crowd in front of the Town Hall.

"There," said Chubb, pointing to a poster that Councillor Stewart Jenvey was pasting up on the Council notice board.

Ginger read it slowly:

IN THE PRESENCE OF
THE RIGHT HONOURABLE PRIME MINISTER
TO CELEBRATE THE BIRTH OF

OUR GREAT COUNTRY
THERE WILL BE A GRAND PARADE
OF THE AUSTRALIAN
ARMY, NAVY, AIR FORCE
TOGETHER WITH
T.V. AND MOVIE STARS,
BUSHRANGERS, SWAGMEN, ROUGHRIDERS
AND OTHERS.

RESIDENTS OF THE DISTRICT
MAY APPLY TO PARTICIPATE

CONTACT S. JENVEY, COUNCILLOR

FOLLOWING THE PARADE
THERE WILL BE A GALA CHARITY SHOW
IN THE TOWN HALL
TICKETS: ADULTS $20
CHILDREN $5

Bennie was the first to speak. "It'll be flabbergasting," he said. "Talk about t'rific!"

"Dead set," agreed Chubb.

"Reckon," said Ginger, his eyes gleaming at the very thought of it. "I'm going to ask Min to go with me. It'll be a top day," he beamed.

"Out of my way, you lot," a loud voice shouted from the back of the crowd. "Make way for a gentleman," it continued grandly. "That's if any of you microbes know what one is."

"Coogan," muttered Ginger.

"The very same, toad features," said Coogan as he squeezed through the crowd, pushing a bright red, brand spanking new wheelbarrow.

"A parade, eh? Big deal!" he said.

No one quite remembered exactly how long Ginger Meggs and Eddie Coogan had been enemies. Ocker Stevens reckoned he remembered Meggsie and Coogan fighting in the maternity wing of the hospital, a couple of days after they were born. It is doubtful that his story can be believed. Ocker was there at the time, but in the cot next to Ginger's. One fact that is reliable, is that both boys have fought each other constantly since kindergarten, when Coogan had used Ginger's face to

demonstrate his finger-painting skill and Ginger in turn had buried Coogan up to his neck in the tots' sandpit just before "sleep time".

They became sworn enemies — a situation that was later made worse when both boys became rivals for the same girlfriend, Jasmin Peters, or Minnie, as she preferred to be called.

The two boys now bristled and faced each other.

"Zoo out for the day, Coogan?" smirked Ginger sarcastically.

"You ought to know, gorilla face," responded Coogan.

Ginger clenched his fist.

By now the crowd was anticipating another of the infamous Meggs–Coogan battles for the paperweight championship of the world.

"Drop the slug, Ginger," urged Bennie.

"Get him, Eddie," countered Darky Nolan, an undersized sycophant who had been following Coogan around on the off chance of getting a ride in his wheelbarrow.

"Go for him, Ginge."

Ginger, spurred on by the crowd's obviously biased support, let fly another insult.

"Thought you'd be out haunting houses, Coogan," he said.

But Coogan, aware that the odds were against him, had decided to slide out of the situation if he could.

"I'd like to take you apart, Meggs, but, lucky for you, I've got better things to do," he said, giving his wheelbarrow a business-like shove.

"Like pushing round that hunk of junk," laughed Ginger, referring to the wheelbarrow.

The Meggs supporters cheered their hero's witty repartee.

"Good one, Ginge," said Bennie.

"Get off it, Meggs. You're just jealous you haven't got one," said Coogan scornfully.

This was so uncomfortably true that for a moment Ginger had no reply.

The loyal Chubb, sensing his trouble, stepped in quickly.

"The way you're acting, y'd reckon it was a Rolls-

Royce instead of a measly old wheelbarrow," said Chubb, pushing past Ginger.

"It's a pity none of you nerds understands anything about aerodyanamics, otherwise you'd realise just how good it is," crowed Coogan. He was relieved. He had managed to shift attention away from the fight. To keep all minds off it, he continued his diversionary chatter.

"My old man designed this so I can wheel *anything, anywhere, any time,* better than *anyone.*"

"Yeah?" said Ginger coolly. "I bet I can wheel something a couple of hundred metres and you won't be able to wheel it back."

"Yeah?" snarled Coogan. "You want to bet?"

"Reckon, turkey," answered Ginger quickly. "What have you got to bet with?"

"What have I got? What have *you* got is more like it," said Coogan, out of the corner of his mouth.

Ginger dug deep into the pockets of his pants. All eyes watched as he dragged out a dirty hankie, two tombolas — slightly chipped — a used bus ticket, an empty chewing-gum packet, a piece of string and, finally, his pride and joy, the Swiss pocket-knife his dad had given him on his last birthday. A prize indeed! Not only did it have three blades and a corkscrew, but, most useful, a gadget to get stones out of horses' hooves or pigs' trotters as well.

To date, Ginger hadn't had cause to use that particular instrument but had not given up hope that somewhere, some day, there'd be a horse or a pig that needed his help.

Ginger proudly held up the pocket-knife for all to see. "I'll bet this," he said confidently.

"THIS!"

There were gasps all round. The thought that Ginger Meggs would stake such a prized possession was almost awesome. It was especially so to Coogan's loyal supporters. Coogan himself was a little taken aback by such a generous offer. His eyes opened wide. His mouth did too.

"Now, what have you got?" asked Ginger.

All eyes turned to Coogan. He slowly reached into the inside pocket of his jacket. He paused, then quickly produced a super large block of nut and raisin chocolate, with only two squares missing. He displayed the treasure arrogantly.

"This!" he shouted, as he held the chocolate above his head.

The crowd was extremely impressed. Little Hookey Hooks, who'd only wandered up to check out the din, became faint at the thought of such a wager.

"You're on, Coogan," said Ginger. "Shake!"

Coogan wiped his hand on Darky Nolan's back, then reluctantly took Ginger's hand. Both boys tried in vain to squeeze the other's hand to pulp.

"Better check your fingers, Ginge," said Bennie. "Count 'em; you can never be too sure when you're dealing with vipers like Coogan."

"Okay, windbag. *Anything* you can wheel, *anywhere*, I can wheel back. It's a bet," said Coogan, confidence oozing from every word.

"That's the bet, Coogan. Darky Nolan here can hold the stakes," said Ginger.

Both objects were handed to Darky.

"Mind you don't eat any," added Coogan threateningly.

Ginger winked at Bennie and Chubb, both of whom looked back at him blankly.

"Tell you what," Ginger turned to Coogan with a nonchalant air, "just to show I've got strength to spare, I'll wheel you a couple of hundred metres as well. Get in!"

There were more exclamations from the chattering gallery, which by now had swelled to a size suitably large for such an important event.

"Suits me, Meggs, I always said you had holes in your head," laughed Coogan as he jumped heavily into the wheelbarrow.

Off went Ginger pushing the wheelbarrow. Off went

27

Bennie, Chubb, Hooks and Nolan. They were just the start of a long procession. There were boys and girls of all shapes and sizes, each as eager as the other to know the outcome of the contest. At the front, Ginger pushed Coogan, who sat like a large galah on his perch in the front of his wheelbarrow.

They passed the police station, where Constable Casey wondered what on earth was going on; they went on by to the statue of the explorer, whose name no one could remember; then down past the pie shop, where half the the crowd were momentarily side-tracked by much-needed refreshments. Then, much to the pleasure of the crowd, they crossed the street and headed back towards Joe's milk bar.

"You're doing okay, Meggsie," snorted Coogan. "If your face didn't make me sick, I'd give you the job permanent like."

"I think maybe, Coogan, you're gonna be sick anyway," said Ginger, turning to wink again at Bennie and Chubb, who were obviously puzzled by his strange behaviour.

Mike and Tony were the first to arrive at the milk bar. They formed a small guard of honour as Ginger wheeled Coogan to the doorway and emptied him out onto the footpath.

"Watch it, Meggs," said Coogan, dusting himself off. "You're joking! This is it? You might as well give me the pocket-knife now!"

"Yeah, this is it," said Ginger confidently. "You see,

"YOU'RE DOING OKAY, MEGGSIE."

I've just wheeled something here, that you can't wheel back. I wheeled YOU!"

"Some joke!" shouted Coogan. "Don't be stupid."

Ginger looked innocently at the crowd.

"Why don't you try wheeling yourself back?" he smiled.

The gallery burst into laughter, which infuriated Coogan. Meggs had made a fool of him in front of half the kids in the district. His face turned red. His nostrils flared. He was speechless.

"Tell him, Darky," said Ginger forcibly.

Darky Nolan took a deep breath; he could forget about getting a ride in the wheelbarrow, unless he wanted to risk the vengeance of the crowd and, worse still, of Ginger Meggs himself.

"It's true, Eddie, you lose," said Darky reluctantly. "You can't wheel yourself back."

More laughter broke out, drowning any further protests Coogan may have had, if he'd been able to talk.

Ginger grabbed the pocket-knife and the chocolate from Darky.

"Come on, you guys," he shouted triumphantly, "the feast's on Coogan."

Coogan was ready to burst. He looked murderously at Ginger. Through clenched teeth he vowed, "I'll get you for this, Meggs. You mark my words. I'll get you."

Ginger laughed and, as usual, ignored Coogan's threats. They were, after all, only a small part of a feller's day.

The chocolate was just about finished when Ginger decided it was time he went home.

"I've got to get there before Mum," he said. "If she finds Fitzcloon cleaning the yard, I'll cop it like mad!"

He quickly set off in the direction of the Meggses' home, with Mike and Tony hot on his heels.

"What a day!" he thought, as he turned into the back lane. "How clever can a feller get? Outsmarting both Fitzcloon and Coogan in the one day! Scoring a freebie bar of chocolate and finding out about the parade and the Prime Minister. Unreal!"

Ginger pushed open the back gate. "Y' luck's turned the corner, Meggsie," he said to himself.

He came to an abrupt halt and stood in amazement. The back yard was unbelievably clean. Even rubbish that had been there for as long as he could remember had been cleared. And there in the centre of the yard was Cuthbert, polishing the clothes line!

Ginger couldn't believe his eyes.

Cuthbert came running up to him.

"I've finished, Ginger. I was just waiting to say thank you! So, thank you, thank you, thank you! You're great! Really great. I'm off to the pool now," he said.

"Boy, do I know some cuckoos," said Ginger to Tony as they watched Cuthbert scramble off down the lane. "He actually thanked me for making him do the yard."

Cuthbert had no sooner disappeared than Mrs Meggs and Dudley came through the back gate.

"Phew!" thought Ginger. "That was close."

"You're still here," said Mrs Meggs. "I thought you'd be at the pool by now."

"Huh?" said Ginger, confused. "Pool?"

Mrs Meggs shook her head. "I'll never understand you," she said. "I left you a note and two dollars under the big straw broom behind the kitchen door, saying that when you'd finished sweeping, you could go to the pool."

The back wire door slammed as she went inside.

Ginger was dumbfounded.

"Two dollars! Two whole dollars! No wonder Fitzcloon carried on the way he did. Now who's the cuckoo?" he thought.

Ginger slumped beside the shiny clothes line. Tony jumped onto his shoulder, and Mike rested his chin on his master's lap.

"Yeah," said Ginger, "Meggs's luck has turned the corner. The corner from bad to worse."

"... THE CORNER FROM BAD TO WORSE."

Chapter 3
Fair Exchange

"**D**EADSET, Bennie," said Ginger earnestly, "so what does Fitzcloon do? Thanks me! Actually thanks me and then with the speed of burning light, racks off down to the pool — clutching my two dollars in his sweaty little piano-playing hands."

Bennie was shocked at Ginger's revelation. Rarely did anyone get the better of Ginger Meggs, let alone a weed like Cuthbert Fitzcloon.

"Humph!" he grunted, and shook his head from side to side. "Tch!"

"It's enough to shake a feller's faith in his fellow man," Ginger muttered.

"Reckon," agreed Bennie.

Ginger and Bennie were sitting on the footpath, leaning against the pole of the "No Standing" sign on their favourite corner. It was a great place to watch the world dawdle by or just to hang out. It was handy to Joe's milk bar, had an uninterrupted three hundred and sixty degree view, so that in case Tiger Kelly happened by there was ample warning to make oneself scarce, and best of all there was always the chance that someone with a spare dollar, who appreciated a feller with a terrible great reputation like Ginger's, might turn up and oblige by shouting a shake or two.

"Two dollars!" mumbled Ginger despondently. He deliberated for a moment. "Could be worse, I s'pose."

Ginger broke into a broad smile and patted Mike on the head.

"At least we ended up with Coogan's chocolate, eh feller?"

Mike yapped loudly.

"Too right!" laughed Bennie.

"AT LEAST WE ENDED UP
WITH COOGAN'S CHOCOLATE..."

"Come on, 'Australia Two'," someone cried noisily, further along the footpath.

"Get off, you can't be 'Australia Two' with a heap of rubbish like that," countered someone else, even louder. "I reckon seeing as mine's winning, it should be 'Australia Two'."

"I said it first. So!"

Ginger turned to see Ocker Stevens and Darky Nolan heading in their direction. They were racing two hastily modelled matchbox boats, with torn beer labels as sails, in the water that trickled down the gutter.

The boxes came to rest against Ginger's foot.

"G'day, Ginger, Bennie!" said Ocker cheerily, as he sat down. "How's it going?"

" 'Day Meggsie," said Darky meekly, not daring to look Ginger directly in the eyes.

"Good thanks, Ock," said Ginger, deliberately ignoring Darky.

He paused, then spoke to Darky out of the corner of his mouth. "Thought you'd be riding around in your mate Coogan's wheelbarrow," he said flatly.

"No way, Ginge, you wouldn't catch me with a creep like Coogan," said Darky, with as much conviction as his squeaky voice would allow. "No, sir, no way, not me."

Ginger stared at him coldly for a moment, then lifted his foot, allowing the challengers to sail on.

"See y', Meggsie," shouted Darky as he hurried after the matchboxes. "You coming, Ock?"

"No, I'm going to hang around with the fellers for a

bit," said Ocker. "You can be 'Australia Two' by yourself."

Darky was tempted to stay. An afternoon in the company of Ginger Meggs was always eventful, if nothing else. Still, yesterday was fresh in both their minds, so he decided to make a speedy exit while he still could. He quickly disappeared around the first corner he came to, leaving both boats to sail on unaccompanied into the whirlpool of the stormwater drain.

"You know, guys, I reckon a feller has got to forget about yesterdays and just think about todays. And it's no use worrying about tomorrows, that's what I reckon," said Ginger profoundly.

"Life's just like one of those matchboxes, one day you're sailing along fine and the next thing you're up to your portholes in a sewer pipe."

"Yeah," said Ocker, awestruck at the depth of Ginger's philosophising.

"Will y' take a look at that!" said Bennie suddenly, ending any chance that Ginger may have had to continue in his deep and meaningful vein. "It looks like Teddy Bader with a...a..."

"A dirty great watermelon," said Ginger and Ocker in unison.

"Wow! Unreal!" exclaimed Bennie.

"Look at the size of it," said Ocker, with equal excitement.

"It's tremendelicious!" added Ginger.

They jumped to their feet and gazed longingly across to the other side of the road, where a smug-looking

"LOOK AT THE SIZE OF IT!"

Teddy Bader was carrying just about the biggest, greenest, juiciest-looking watermelon anyone could ever remember seeing.

Ocker's eyes widened. It was a well-known fact that Ocker Stevens's favourite thing in the whole world was fresh watermelon, and on a hot day like today, it was asking too much of him to suggest he forget it. His tongue travelled slowly around the outside of his mouth as he watched, mesmerised, as the watermelon got closer.

Bennie sat down again.

"It's no use. Teddy Bader wouldn't give you a used match, let alone a bit of his watermelon," he groaned.

Ocker's face dropped. Unfortunately what Bennie was saying was true. He slumped to the footpath.

"Of all the people lucky enough to score a watermelon, it had to be Bader," muttered Ocker, resigned to savouring only the sight of the green striped delicacy.

Tony sat next to him and squeaked in sympathy, for watermelon was his favourite too.

Ginger stood with his hands on his hips and grinned at his doleful-looking companions. *He* wasn't about to give up that easily. There was no reason to chuck in the sponge, just because a feller had a reputation for being as tight as a lifesaver's T-shirt. A watermelon, after all, was made big enough to share. If it were an apple or a pear that Bader was so proudly displaying, he might be permitted to scoff it by himself. But a watermelon, and especially one that size, was destined to be enjoyed *en masse,* and Ginger was determined to be part of that *masse.*

"You never know," said Ginger, with a gleam in his eyes. "I reckon even a tightwad like Bader could be persuaded into sharing, especially if his watermelon was busted into pieces."

He grinned slyly. His freckles turned a deeper shade of red.

"I've got a plan," he said. "Operation Melon! Follow me!"

Ginger bolted off, with Mike and Tony at his heels.

"Well, come on," said Ocker enthusiastically, leaping to his feet. Whatever Ginger's plan was, it was worth a try.

Teddy Bader regarded himself as careful in all matters concerning money and personal possessions. Whether he could justifiably be called a "tightwad" was open to debate, though the tarnished fifty-cent piece, his first ever weekly allowance, framed and proudly displayed over his bed, may have tipped the scales against him.

His father, an assistant manager at the local branch of the State Bank, had taught him to be frugal; so frugal he was. It didn't matter what the likes of wastrels like Ginger Meggs or Ocker Stevens or Bennie Hooper did or said, the joy of his bulging piggy bank easily outweighed the scorn of their infantile remarks.

Bader, now whistling his way along the street under the weight of the enormous melon, had no idea that at the next corner waited a band as desperate as any that had ever existed.

A thatch of red merged with the shadows that fell across the old sandstone wall.

"Now, here's what we're going to do," whispered Ginger. "When Bader reaches the corner, we all run out, as if we've been racing; and if my calculations are correct, the point of impact should be somewhere about there." He pointed to a small crack a metre or so from the corner.

"Crash!" continued Ginger. "And down will go watermelon, Bader and all! As everyone knows, it's impossible to carry home a zillion bits of melon, so we'll all just have to eat it."

He gave the thumbs-up sign.

Bennie and Ocker were all smiles. Mike wagged his tail briskly, while Tony gave a squeal of monkey approval.

"Shush," commanded Ginger, moving deeper into the shadow. "He's coming."

The whistling and slow footsteps grew louder. The final countdown for "Operation Melon" was under way.

Ginger marshalled his troops. "Ready, on y' marks, set," he paused and took a deep breath, "go!"

Ginger's timing was impeccable. Just as Bader reached the corner, so did the onslaught.

Crunch! Bang! Thump!

"Argh!" cried Bader as he found himself travelling through the air in the opposite direction.

Thud!

He skidded to a stop and ended bottom side up against an empty "Be Tidy" bin.

"Oops, sorry, Teddy," said Ginger, trying his hardest to look concerned, but failing miserably. "I do beg your pardon. You're not hurt, I hope?"

Bader looked up through a sea of swirling stars to see not one, but two, red-headed blurs looking down at him. He blinked slowly, trying to focus on the grinning heads that gradually dissolved into one.

"M...m...m...Meggsie?" he stammered, through the sounds of pealing church bells and chirruping bluebirds that were coming from inside his head. As far as he knew he'd been hit by a speeding train or, at the very least, a semi-trailer.

Meanwhile, much to everyone's amazement, the watermelon had failed to shatter and right at that moment was bouncing at a great pace down the street as though possessed of a will of its own.

40

Ginger could hardly believe it.

"Impossible," he said. "Don't just stand there, you guys, let's get it."

The chase was on.

The melon gained momentum and the excitement grew as the melon-chasers closed in.

Mike had charged to the front of the bunch by three lengths and was gaining fastest on the melon.

"Go for it, feller," shouted Ginger, in full stride.

Mike took a gigantic leap and landed on top of the runaway.

Cheers went up from the pursuing posse.

But their joy was momentary. The sheer weight and speed of the renegade fruit bowled the bewildered pup backwards, and into the path of the pursuers. A major collision was narrowly avoided only by some fancy footwork.

"Would y' believe it," said Ginger. "It's fighting back."

"Stop, melon," shouted Ocker, in his most commanding tone. But the watermelon bounced obliviously on.

An extraordinary spurt of speed saw Bennie come within millimetres of the fugitive fruit.

"Dive, Bennie, dive," shouted Ginger. "Tackle it!"

Bennie launched himself horizontally, in copybook fashion, threw both arms around the watermelon and squeezed. For a fleeting moment he had it.

Then, pop! The shiny melon shot straight out of his

grasp and continued on, even faster than before.

Ginger had almost drawn level with the speeding watermelon when it suddenly hit a stone and flew high into the air.

The chase came to a standstill as everyone stood and watched.

Up and up went the watermelon. Higher and higher. For a moment it appeared to stop and hang suspended in space before beginning its rapid descent.

"Mine!" shouted Ginger, positioning himself for the catch of the season. But he had slightly misjudged the melon's arc and, rather than falling into Ginger's waiting arms, it fell slap bang into the centre of a nearby open manhole where two unsuspecting Telecom employees were heatedly discussing whose turn it was to work next.

"What the . . .!" boomed from beneath the footpath.

"Gee!" chorused the breathless group as they stared down into the abyss.

No one really knew what to say or what to do.

Ginger shrugged. He'd take control of the situation.

"Hey, mister! You, down there. Will you chuck us up our watermelon, please?" he asked, as politely as possible.

There was no answer. The boys looked at each other, concerned at the lack of response.

"It might have killed 'em," said Ocker, looking worried.

Ginger considered the possibility and shook his head. Then, "Go on, mister," he pleaded, "chuck it up."

Still nothing. A note of desperation crept into his voice. "Is there anyone down there?" he asked hesitantly.

Finally, a deep voice rose from the depths.

"Beat it," it said gruffly.

Ocker breathed a sigh of relief. At least someone was alive.

"Can we have our watermelon, please?" he said.

"What watermelon?" laughed a second voice.

"Aw, fair go," said Bennie.

"Yes, come off it," said Ginger, "we saw where it went."

"I didn't see no watermelon, Sid," said the first voice. "Did you see a watermelon?"

"No, Merv, I didn't see no watermelon either," answered the second voice. "Then again, maybe they mean the one we're gonna have for lunch."

"Could be, Sid. Could be," said the first voice.

The little gang stood silently and stared into the hole. They were all too aware of what had happened and, worse still, what was about to happen.

The first voice spoke again. "If you kids want to hang around for a while," it said, "we'll chuck you some skins to chew on."

Laughter echoed from the manhole into the street.

Ocker groaned as an exhausted Teddy Bader arrived on the scene.

"Sorry for bumping into you, Teddy, and losing your watermelon," said Ginger. The misery in his voice was more for the loss of the melon than the bruising of Bader.

"Don't worry about me, Ginger," said Bader, "just explain it to your mum."

"Huh?" said Ginger. "*My* mum?"

Bader continued, in the tone of a teacher instructing a class.

"She sent me for it," he said. "It was supposed to be a surprise for you," and Bader swung off down the footpath.

Ginger went weak at the knees.

Bennie shook his head, unable to speak.

"Um, er..." mumbled Ocker, his face blank.

They turned back to the blackness of the manhole, from which the sounds of slurping and the smacking of lips rose to torment them.

"*My* watermelon," mumbled Ginger sadly. "*Mine!*"

"After all that running, too," said Ocker.

"I'd even be happy with an orange now," said Bennie. "You should have seen the ones Tiger Kelly was picking for Mr Foster this morning."

Ginger sat up alertly.

"Tiger Kelly's working in Foster's orchard?" he said.

"If you can call what Kelly does, work," grinned Bennie. "He was there when I came past on my way to your place."

"Unreal!" said Ginger. "I could go an orange myself."

"You had more chance of separating Bader from the watermelon than you'd have of extracting an orange from Tiger Kelly," said Ocker.

"And you couldn't be beaten to a pulp by Bader," said Bennie.

It was no use talking. Ginger had made up his mind. If he couldn't have watermelon, he was going to have oranges, and that was that.

"Hey, you guys," he shouted down the manhole, "I thought you were going to give us some skins to chew on."

The gravel-like voice once again rose from the depths. "You asked for it, kid!" it said.

A hail of skins spewed out of the manhole like lava from an erupting volcano.

Ginger started to pick them up. "Thanks, mister," he said. "Come on, you guys. Grab as many as you can, then let's find Tiger Kelly."

"You really are going to look for Tiger Kelly?" muttered Bennie.

"You must definitely be sick of living, or something," said Ocker, equally stunned at Ginger's outrageous suggestion.

"Trust me," smiled Ginger. "A feller knows what he's doing."

Bennie and Ocker formed a step with their hands so that Ginger was able to look over the fence that surrounded Foster's orchard.

He could see no sign of Tiger Kelly. There were plenty of juicy, ripe oranges, but no orange-picker.

"He must have knocked off," he said.

As he spoke, Ginger noticed a slight movement beneath one of the trees in the far corner. That had to be Tiger. The shape moved again. It was him. Curled up and sound asleep was the infamous Tiger Kelly. The scourge of little kids, the terror of old ladies.

"He's there all right," said Ginger excitedly.

"Oh!" chorused Bennie and Ocker, less than happy with the news of the discovery.

"He's sleeping, just like a baby," whispered Ginger.

"Some baby!" moaned Bennie.

"I reckon I can get him from here," said Ginger. "Get me the biggest, squashiest bit of watermelon skin you can find."

They quickly sorted through the pieces until they found exactly what Ginger had asked for.

"Good," said Ginger.

Ginger balanced himself carefully on the fence. He took aim at the unsuspecting target. Slowly his arm came back. He glanced apprehensively at Bennie and Ocker. Then as hard as he could he let fly with the skin.

Splosh! Right on target. Smack on the back of Tiger's head.

Tiger woke with a scream.

" 'Bout time you did a bit of work, isn't it, *Mr* Kelly," said Ginger defiantly.

The seconds ticked by. Tiger gathered his thoughts. It slowly dawned on him what had happened.

"Why, Meggsie, you microbe," he scowled. "You wait!"

Tiger bent down, picked up the nearest orange and flung it ferociously at Ginger.

Ginger ducked in time and the projectile whistled past his left ear.

"Missed!" tormented Ginger. "You're getting old, Tige."

"Yeah," roared Tiger, "try this one for size."

A second orange whizzed by. Then a third.

"You need more practice, Tiger!" jibed Ginger. Then out of the corner of his mouth, "Grab 'em."

"Practice, eh?" spluttered Tiger. "We'll see who needs practice, microbe!"

Ginger ducked and weaved precariously on the fence as orange after orange flew by, while below, Bennie, Ocker and Tony gathered up the spent missiles.

"We've got enough, Ginger," said Bennie, overjoyed at the unexpected windfall.

"Right," said Ginger. "Well, Tiger," he continued, "I'd like to be able to stick around to give you target practice, but I'd better be off. Wouldn't want to stop you working."

" SPLOSH ! "

Tiger darted swiftly towards the fence.

"You're dead, Meggs," he bellowed.

"You here, Kelly?" called Mr Foster, from amidst the orange trees.

Tiger screeched to a stop.

Mr Foster continued, "Where are you, Kelly? If you're not working, you're fired!"

Tiger hurriedly began packing oranges into the nearest box he could find.

"H...h...here, m...m...Mr Foster," he stuttered. "Er, j...just about finished."

He turned and glared at Ginger, "You'll keep, Meggsie!"

"See y' round, Tige," said Ginger, leaping down to the footpath where his mates were loaded up with the results of Tiger's unintentional generosity.

"Let's get stuck into them," said Ginger, puffing his chest out. "Watermelon for oranges, it's a fair exchange, if you ask me."

There was no way Ginger was going to get any argument from his contented companions.

Chapter 4
The Champ

EDDIE Coogan had spent a sleepless night, tossing and turning, trying to think of some way to get even with Ginger for the humiliation he had suffered over the wheelbarrow incident.

This time Meggs had gone too far. No one made Coogan the laughing stock of the neighbourhood and got away with it. Especially Meggs! He'd be made to pay, and pay dearly.

Coogan could, of course, challenge his red-headed rival to a man-to-man, public, super showdown, a brawl to end all brawls, an official contest complete with a referee. A clash that Gawler's Paddock would never forget. It would decide once and for all who was boss cocky of the district.

Unfortunately it also meant playing by the rules, which meant that Coogan stood a good chance of coming off second best and would then have to endure a lifetime of embarrassment.

"No," he thought. "Dealing with the likes of Ginger

Meggs calls for far more subtle action. Something safe, shrewd and sneaky. The sneakier the better."

Coogan found himself knocking on Jug Ears Jonson's door. Under normal circumstances he wouldn't have been within kilometres of the place, but, where revenge was concerned, nothing was too much to endure, not even an afternoon with Jug Ears.

Politely stated, Jug Ears Jonson hadn't been endowed with an abundance of brains. Added to this he had the personality of a jar of jam. Without a doubt he was the most boring kid on the block. But whatever he lacked in brightness he more than made up for in physical size and strength.

He also had a reputation as a "terrible great fighter". Through pure gall or lack of nous, no one was quite sure which, he actually took on Tiger Kelly one afternoon on the way home from school. Not that Jug Ears was into fighting; he much preferred eating. And in fact the fight with Tiger had been over an "*après* class" bag of lollies owned by Jug Ears for a very short while before Tiger relieved him of them. Jug Ears, of course, was beaten to a pulp, but during the scuffle he actually managed to land two hefty punches on Kelly. Two more than anyone else had been able to before or since.

To date, Jug Ears Jonson and Ginger Meggs had barely crossed each other's paths, let alone had cause to test each other's pugilistic skills. Though it was generally acknowledged by local pundits that Jug Ears's distinct height and weight advantage would be the telling factor and that fisticuffs between the two would have been worth witnessing.

But Ginger wisely kept a diplomatic distance between himself and the overly large Master Jonson, and Jug Ears was happy to have it that way. He sought no quarrel with anyone. He let his reputation take care of him and, on the odd occasion, usually around luchtime, he'd give a weed like Darky Nolan or Clocker Burns a long, lingering, icy stare which was always sufficient to coax the agreeable offer of half their sandwiches from them. It was much easier than having to thump anybody.

Coogan knew that his task would be difficult, but he was determined to succeed. The Jonson door slowly creaked open. Jug Ears appeared. With his usual lifeless expression and monotone voice, he asked, "What do you want, ferret face?"

Coogan realised he'd have to act quickly if his plan was to succeed.

"I was . . . er . . . was, just passing," he said, obviously unsure of what to say next, " . . . er . . . when I wondered if . . . er . . . you were home."

"So?"

"I thought if anyone . . . er . . . would be happy to share my good . . . er . . . fortune, it'd be good ol' Jug Ears Jonson."

Jug Ears was unmoved. Coogan could see he was losing ground. This was going to be even harder than he had envisaged.

"Good fortune! That is, this top packet of jelly beans my nanna gave me," he said, producing a packet marked "Extra Black Ones".

"Hmm," Jug Ears pondered, nodding his head and almost smiling.

Coogan sighed with relief. It wasn't much of a reaction but at least he was beginning to get through. He continued, far more confidently.

"Yeah, I thought. The one guy that would really appreciate a bag of jelly beans like this would be my ol' mate Jug Ears. So, here I am." Coogan held out the bag of sweets.

Jug Ears smiled broadly and extended his hand. Coogan filled it to capacity with the jelly beans and watched in amazement as the entire load disappeared in one gulp down the chasm of Jug Ears's mouth.

As far as Jug Ears was concerned, anyone who was

"GOOD DAY, JUG EARS, OLD MATE."

willing to share his lollies, unsolicited, was a friend indeed.

"Great stuff," said Jug Ears. "Come inside, I've been smashing up some old plastic soldiers I didn't want anymore. You can help me."

Coogan took a deep breath then stepped inside.

"Sure thing, mate," he said. "I'd love to. Here, have a black one."

He pushed the door shut with his foot, and smiled to himself. He knew revenge was only a matter of hours away.

"Are these oranges any good, or are they any good?" said Ginger contentedly, smacking his lips.

The others were far too busy chomping, sucking and slurping to answer properly. Their orange-stained mouths and juice-soaked clothes said it all.

It wasn't long before the morning's cleverly gotten gains had been reduced to a large, sticky pile of skins and pips.

"Talk about giving a guy an appetite," said Ocker, rubbing his stomach with delight. "Think I'll go home and see what Mum's burnt for lunch."

"Yeah, me too," said Bennie. "Oranges sure make y' hungry."

"You're not wrong," said Ginger as he gulped down the last remaining quarter of orange. "Think I'll wander over to Min's, they always have a good spread there and I can tell her about the Australia Day procession and the Prime Minister and everything."

Ginger grinned at his two friends. "Anyway," he said, "I think we were supposed to have watermelon at our place."

The little group deposited the remains of the mid-morning repast in the nearest "Be Tidy" bin, then briskly headed off to their different destinations.

"Race y'," said Ginger to Mike and Tony as they reached the wrought-iron gates of the park. "Last one to the east entrance is an old mother hen. Ready, set . . . go!"

"Hey, Ginge," screamed a voice from behind them. The urgency in its tone stopped Ginger and Tony in their tracks and brought Mike, who was five metres up the path, to a screeching halt.

"Am I glad I found you!" It was a white-faced, out-of-breath, panicking Chubb who hurried up to Ginger. "Phew!" he gasped. "Are you *lucky* I found you!"

"Why? What's up, Chubb?" enquired Ginger.

"It's . . . it's Coogan, he's looking for y'," he said, still trying to catch his breath.

"So let him find me," responded Ginger casually. "When did you last see me worry about that turkey?"

"It's not him you have to worry about, Ginge," said Chubb gravely. "It's . . . " he paused, "Jug Ears Jonson! He's with Coogan. They're after you."

"Oh, get off it!" said Ginger, but it was obvious Chubb's message had him worried. "What would Jug Ears be doing with Coogan? And anyway, he's got no reason to want to bash me. I haven't spoken to him for ages."

"IT'S... JUG EARS JONSON!"

"You mightn't have spoken to him," said Chubb, "but Coogan has. I bumped into Hookey Hooks who reckoned Darky Nolan told him that he'd spoken to both Coogan and Jug Ears and they'd told him they were going to spread you over the footpath like Vegemite over a bit of toast."

"Uh oh." Ginger paled.

"Hookey said Coogan was really cheesed off about the wheelbarrow yesterday and was going to get you for it. According to Darky, he filled Jug Ears up with jelly beans and pretended they were good mates."

"The viper," mumbled Ginger, his head sinking further into his shoulders each time Chubb spoke.

"Then, when Coogan had Jug Ears in the palm of his slimy little paw, he tells him you reckoned you could take

58

Jug Ears apart with one arm tied behind your back, and the reason you two had never fought each other until now was because he was an overblown chicken!"

Ginger groaned. "Surely not even Jug Ears would fall for a story like that," he said.

"Would you believe a guy busy stuffing you with free jelly beans and pretending he was the best friend you had in the whole world?" said Chubb.

Ginger nodded reluctantly.

"And there's more!" said Chubb.

"More?" spluttered Ginger disbelievingly.

"Yeah. Coogan also told Jug Ears that you said he might have the strength of an elephant but he had the brains of one as well."

"Uh oh."

"And . . . "

"And? There's still more?" said Ginger, his voice fading as he spoke.

"Coogan confided in his new-found best friend, that he'd once overheard you telling the kids at school that you knew for sure that Mrs Jonson had adopted Jug Ears from a wildlife sanctuary. You can imagine the temper Jug Ears was in after that. Darky Nolan reckoned he turned purple, but that might have been because he got a jelly bean stuck in his throat while Coogan was telling him."

Ginger slumped limply to the footpath. It was one thing to have Tiger Kelly after your blood, but definitely a different kettle of fish to have an aggravated Jug Ears hunting you, especially when his reasoning had been poisoned by a snake-in-the-grass like Eddie Coogan.

"Anyway, I thought you had better know," said Chubb sincerely.

"Thanks, mate," said Ginger. "A feller ought to know when his life's on the line, whether he wants to or not."

"What are you going to do?" asked Chubb.

"Check Mum's got the Medicare card handy," said Ginger, looking sick already.

Chubb failed to see the joke.

"Yeah," he said quietly.

"Anyway," said Ginger, "I'm on my way to Min's . . ."

"I wouldn't go through the park!" interrupted Chubb. "I reckon that's where they'll be. Coogan's got Darky Nolan keeping a lookout near your place too."

"Trust that weed," mumbled Ginger. "I should have sent him down the river with his matchbox."

Ginger could imagine Jug Ears's enraged face glaring at him. He remembered a time when Jug Ears had pulled the head off an old rag doll he'd found in the playground. The more Ginger thought about it the more the doll resembled him, red hair and all.

"You all right, Ginger?" asked Chubb, concerned. He'd never seen Ginger look so dazed.

"No worries," said Ginger, as the horrible vision disappeared. "I won't go by the park, I'll go to Min's the back way, down Leckie Street."

Chubb's eyes opened wide. He couldn't believe what he was hearing.

"Leckie Street!"

It was unthinkable that anyone in their right mind

would go anywhere near Leckie Street, let alone down it, even to avoid the awesome temper of someone like Jug Ears Jonson. It was well known that, tough as he thought he was, Tiger Kelly had never dared set foot in Leckie Street and that even Constable Casey avoided Leckie Street whenever possible.

Of all the streets in the district, Leckie Street was the roughest, toughest and meanest. It was always dark, damp and smelly, even on a hot summer's day.

Ginger could see the look of amazement on Chubb's face.

"I have to see Min, while I'm still able to," said Ginger despondently, "so I don't have much choice."

"But Leckie Street?" gasped Chubb.

"I reckon I've got more of a chance there, especially if I run flat out. Anyway, it mightn't be as bad as everyone makes out. After all, no one that we know has ever been down there," said Ginger.

"Not that's lived to tell about it," said Chubb, half to himself.

"What else can I do?"

Chubb was still stunned but agreed with Ginger's logic.

"I've got to go home for lunch," he said reluctantly. "The oldies are having some friends over and I have to play with their kid, otherwise I'll be in for it. I'll see you later this arvo," said Chubb. "Either at your place or the hospital," he added dolefully.

"Yeah," said Ginger glumly.

Ginger reached the corner that led into the notorious Leckie Street. Slowly and carefully he poked his head around the crumbling brick wall that marked the start of the street. At his feet Mike and Tony poked their heads around the wall as well.

"Well, all I can say is, if I'm not scared, this is the nearest I've been to it," Ginger mumbled under his breath.

He looked longingly towards the sunny far end of the street and sighed. Between him and safety stretched a minefield of overturned garbage tins, broken bottles, rusted cans, newspapers blowing along in the breeze, wrecked cars, tumbledown old terraced houses and wall after wall of graffiti. Strange, muffled noises were coming from the houses.

It was the stuff of which nightmares are made. At first glance the street appeared to be deserted.

"Maybe it's some sort of Leckie Street holiday. They might all be at a picnic," thought Ginger, trying to buck himself up but certain that somewhere in the shadows lurked danger.

Ginger took a couple of hesitant paces along the footpath. There was a loud crash behind him. His heart leapt into his mouth; Tony leapt on his back. He turned quickly, just in time to see the scruffiest, most war-torn, flea-bitten alley cat he had ever laid eyes on, disappearing into a side lane. Hanging out of its mouth was an old fish head it had scavenged out of one of the upturned garbage bins.

Ginger breathed a long sigh of relief and edged his

way yet further into the darkness. With every step he became more uncertain. Maybe it *was* a mistake taking a short cut through Leckie Street. Then he remembered: what choice *did* he have? At least there was a slim chance he could make it this way, whereas somewhere behind him was certain bodily harm at the hands of Jug Ears Jonson.

He looked down at Mike and Tony.

"We've got to make a run for it," he whispered. "It's the only way. Watch out for the broken bottles."

Mike whimpered and wagged his tail without noticeable enthusiasm.

"Get ready, I'll tell you when."

Ginger crept a few more metres along the street. Mike and Tony followed closely at his heels.

"Okay, stand by," he said. Then, to reassure them and himself, he grinned and added, "Last one there's an old mother hen."

Ginger took a deep breath and was about to attempt a record-breaking dash when . . .

"'Ere, you," roared an unfriendly voice from the shadows. "Whad do y' think you're doin' in our street, wimp?"

Ginger looked up. Glowering in front of him was a hulking brute with a cigarette balanced delicately from the corner of his bottom lip. He lurched towards Ginger.

"I . . . I . . . I . . . " spluttered Ginger; his feet seemed Superglued to the ground. "I . . . I . . . I . . . "

Mike and Tony hid behind Ginger's legs.

"Well, can't y' talk? Dumb or sumpthin'?"

Ginger shook his head.

"You got a passport?" laughed the stranger.

Ginger shook his head again.

"In that case, pickle-puss, I'm going to knock your ears off, see."

The brute grabbed Ginger by the collar and lifted him off the ground. Ginger shut his eyes, anticipating the worst. Suddenly, another voice penetrated the darkness.

"Whad do y' think y' doing, Pig's Head?" the voice said slowly.

Ginger opened his eyes to see a second ruffian shuffle up to where he hung suspended from Pig's Head's fist. Hope registered on Ginger's face. As far as he could make out the second guy looked pretty much the same as the first, except for a tattoo of a skull and crossbones on his hand. But tattoo or no tattoo, a rescuer in any shape or form was more than welcome.

"Whad are y' doin'?" Ginger's tattooed knight repeated.

"What's it to you, Muscles?" came the sarcastic reply and Ginger was dropped on his bottom on the footpath.

"You're not going to thump that kid!"

Ginger looked up and smiled — saved in the nick of time!

"Oh yeah?"

"Yeah," said Muscles. "I'm going to thump him."

Ginger's smile dropped like a lead balloon. Looking up he saw the two meanest faces he could ever remember seeing, while awake, and the owners of both seemed equally determined to relocate his ears.

"And who says you're going to thump him?" snapped Pig's Head.

"This does," and Muscles let fly and landed an almighty punch. Wham! The sound echoed around the street.

"Argh!" screamed Pig's Head as he flew back and landed in a nearby pile of rubbish.

Ginger, Mike and Tony jumped for cover behind a stack of empty cardboard cartons.

Muscles looked around to see where they had gone and in doing so failed to notice his opponent stumble groggily back from the garbage. He felt a tap on the shoulder. As he turned, a fist came heavily in contact with his chin. He bounced off the lamp post in front of Ginger and straight back into the fray.

Sock!

Whack!

Thump!

Crash!

Both youths flew at each other like a pair of roosters in a chicken coop.

The pair crashed to the gutter and rolled into a lane nearby, squashing the alley cat that was quietly trying to finish off the fish head. Then they rolled back into Leckie Street and were up and into it again.

A wrinkled face popped out from an upstairs window, yawned and popped back inside. Ginger, rooted to the spot, watched in amazement.

By now both fighters were suffering first-degree bleeding noses and were minus a tooth or two. Their punching was becoming less frenzied and noticeably weaker as they attempted to support each other long enough to get a hit in.

Muscles went down on his knees. Pig's Head took aim, wound up and let fly with a haymaker. Before he could make contact, his opponent fell to the ground. Pig's Head's fist, having missed its intended target, continued its lethal arc then landed right in the centre of his own face. His eyes rolled upwards, his knees gave way and he crashed to the footpath.

The street was again dark and quiet.

Ginger was agape. Could this really be happening? He came out from behind the boxes and slowly tiptoed to the scene of the fierce battle. Never in all his days of fighting had he seen anything like this.

He prodded one ruffian. He was out cold! He bent down and prodded the other. He was also out cold!

"Would you believe it, they're both knocked out! I never would have believed it if I hadn't seen it." Ginger whistled in amazement and then turned the whistle into a cheeky tune as he gathered up Tony and gave Mike a reassuring pat. He was just about to set off again when from the end of Leckie Street came a call:

"Hey, Meggs, ferret face."

Ginger knew the voice. It was Jug Ears Jonson.

He turned slowly. Sure enough, there was the third meanest face he'd seen that day, and next to it, grinning like a hungry hyena, was Coogan.

Next to him, looking just about as hungry, were two of Coogan's weeds who had tagged along to watch the promised destruction of Ginger Meggs.

"Good day, Jug Ears," said Ginger cheerily, trying to look as unconcerned as possible.

"It's not good for you, Meggs," interrupted Coogan. Then, realising he may have overstepped the mark, he turned to Jug Ears and said, "Is it, mate?"

Jug Ears curled up the corner of his mouth, narrowed his eyes, and somehow popped his eyes.

"Too right, it's not," he said.

Ginger could feel his mouth drying. He tried to swallow and almost choked. He took a step to the side and in doing so, revealed the awful scene of the two Leckie Street youths lying groaning and bleeding in the gutter.

"Gosh! Look at what Meggs has done!" cried one of the weeds.

"Gee, he's skittled both of them," said the other.

Ginger noticed the look of horror flash across Jug Ears's face.

"Well, I don't let anybody get tough with me," he said, as casually and as coolly as he was able to, under the circumstances.

Jug Ears looked wide-eyed at Coogan, who stood speechless, and shrugged. His jaw dropped to his chest.

"Gee!" he gasped, transfixed by the two figures on the ground. "Gee!"

"You were looking for me?" said Ginger theatrically.

Coogan stepped forward and was about to speak when Jug Ears grabbed him roughly by the shoulders and pulled him back.

"Er . . . what I was saying was, it's no use two great fighters, like us, being enemies," said Jug Ears. "We ought to be friends."

"Huh!" said Coogan.

Jug Ears continued, "Yeah, friends! My mate Eddie here was saying just that this morning. 'We ought to find Ginger Meggs so I can shout us all a shake at Joe's.' Didn't you say that Eddie?"

"I did?" squeaked Coogan, looking helplessly at Jug Ears towering above him. "I did!"

"Well, if you put it like that, Jug, I don't see how I can refuse you. Come on, I know a short cut," beamed Ginger triumphantly.

Chapter 5
Tiger Takes the Cake

"**R**EALLY unreal!" said Ginger, wiping his hand across his mouth. "I've always said Joe makes the best shakes in the world, and when Coogan pays, they taste even better!"

There was muffled laughter all round. Everyone agreed. Everyone, that is, except Coogan, who gave a forced smile and continued to chew on the end of his straw.

He hadn't really heard a word of what Ginger had said. His thoughts were elsewhere. He was already busy hatching another plot to get even with his arch enemy. At this stage he wasn't sure what, when or where he would do it, but one thing was certain, Meggs was going to suffer more than he'd ever suffered before.

"C'mon, Eddie, you haven't touched yours yet," bellowed Jug Ears, eyeing off Coogan's shake, at the same time managing to shove the huge blob of ice-cream onto the end of his straw and into his mouth where he swallowed it in one gulp.

"WHEN COOGAN PAYS, THEY TASTE EVEN BETTER!"

"I'm not really thirsty," muttered Coogan. That was all Jug Ears needed to hear. In fact, it was exactly what he'd been hoping to hear. Before Coogan was able to utter another word, Jug Ears had reached across the counter and, with the speed of greased lightning, grabbed the untouched milk shake.

Coogan sat dumbfounded, dazed by the swiftness of the normally slow-moving Jug Ears. His straw dangled out of his mouth and dripped onto the counter.

"Well, no use wasting this," continued Jug Ears. "Here, Meggsie, we'll go halves." He poured half of Coogan's shake into Ginger's empty container.

Coogan was flabbergasted! If injury had ever been

added to insult, this was it. He stared sternly at Ginger who by now was sucking as noisily as he could on his straw.

It was more than Coogan was prepared to take. He hopped down from the stool and headed towards the door.

"Not going, are you, Edward?" remarked Ginger with wicked politeness.

Coogan paused momentarily without changing his expression.

"Yeah, Eddie, don't go yet. I thought you said you were coming back to my place for the arvo," said Jug Ears.

Coogan's face flushed in mild panic as he floundered around for a legitimate-sounding excuse.

His mind was ticking over like a city taxi meter. This was a delicate situation. He didn't want to upset Jug Ears and run the risk of getting flattened; then again the day had been disastrous enough without having to spend the rest of the afternoon with the "most boring kid on the block".

"I just remembered there are a couple of things my mum wanted me to do," said Coogan, trying to sound as sincere and as disappointed as possible.

"Never mind," said Jug Ears. "Come around tomorrow."

"Yeah, maybe tomorrow," answered Coogan, attempting to sound as eager as possible.

"Don't forget you have to give Darky Nolan a go in your wheelbarrow for watching Meggsie's place this morning," said Jug Ears innocently.

Ginger and Coogan glared at each other.

"I'll be seeing you around too, Meggs," Coogan blustered. "And if I was you, I would worry."

The sudden noisy suction sound of Jug Ears guzzling the final few drops of milk shake, oblivious to all around him, ended the confrontation. Coogan turned sharply and crashed into the side of the shop entrance, momentarily knocking the wind out of himself.

"Hey you, Mister Coogan, watcha the door, eh!" said Joe from behind the counter. "Whata you break, you paya for, okay?"

The milk bar erupted into laughter.

Coogan dusted himself off, looked coldly at everyone laughing, then stormed out into the street.

"Funny feller, that Coogan, eh, Meggsie?" said Jug Ears. "Do anything for a laugh!"

"Yeah!" said Ginger. "Anything!"

Ginger ran his straw around the bottom of the milk shake container, making sure every dreg was gone.

"That just about does me," he said, jumping down from the counter stool. "It's been real, Jug, real real!"

"Want to come back to my place this arvo, Meggsie?" said Jug Ears. "I'm mashing up some old plastic trucks I don't want any more and there's still a couple of jelly beans we could bog into that Coogan left me."

Ginger politely resisted Jug Ears's tempting offer. He pointed to the old grease-covered clock above the hamburger sign.

"Can't, Jug, ol' mate," he said, "as much as I'd like to. I've got to get over to Minnie Peters's place. There's something important I have to ask her. I'm late already. Another time maybe."

"Whatever you say, Meggsie," said Jug Ears, a little downhearted.

Ginger called to Mike and Tony.

"See y' round, Jug."

Jug Ears grunted and pondered over his lot. How come everyone kept putting off coming to his place until "another time"? It seemed that every kid in town, except him, was always busy. Still, that left him time for a bit of eating...

"Double chocolate, double milk, double malt," he shouted across the counter to Joe.

Ginger soon found himself back at the old wrought-iron gate that marked the entrance to the park.

"I reckon we've missed lunch at the Peterses',"he said, "so I guess the oranges and shakes will just have to do us until tonight."

The threesome was striding purposefully through the park when Ginger noticed an unusual scene. Herbie Haeburn and his young brother Normie were engrossed in what appeared to be a deep and meaningful conversation; at least it was on Herbie's part, since he was doing all the talking while Normie stood rigid, apparently trying to take it all in. Now, it is not often that a big brother takes time in a busy schedule to talk to a little brother. But there was Herbie in full throttle — his arms waving vigorously about, his fingers being pointed deftly at imaginary objects and his clenched fists periodically being thrust into the air. This needed investigation, or certainly, Ginger decided, it warranted closer inspection.

"Ah, there, Herbie, good day," said Ginger. "What are you up to?"

"Important stuff, Meggsie," answered Herbie seriously, "I'm going to teach my young brother, Normie, the greatest lesson in life!"

Ginger wasn't too sure what Herbie was on about. However, seeing that Herbie always managed to come in the top three at school, the wisest thing he could do would be to agree with him, otherwise a guy could end up looking like a fool in front of the young feller.

"You can't teach 'em too young, Herbie," said Ginger assuredly. Then, noticing that Herbie hadn't detected his charade, added, "Life's liable to be pretty rough sometimes."

"Exactly, Ginge, that's just what I've been telling Normie. Now, take me, Ginge. You're looking at a feller that knows what it's like to be kicked from pillar to parking meter."

Herbie stopped talking just long enough to draw breath, which was fine by Ginger, who still didn't have the slightest idea where the conversation was leading.

"It's up to an older brother . . ." Herbie began waving his arm frantically in the air again " . . . to protect an innocent kid in a terrible hard world."

No sooner had Herbie stopped than he was off again.

"Corky Stenning. There's a case! I lend him two dollars, need it back, down on my knees I go to him, but not one cent do I get. Gone with the wind it is!"

Ginger could do little except grunt the occasional "yeah" and "reckon" at appropriate intervals.

"And Peanut Perkins," continued Herbie intently, "I lent him a couple of top cassettes. I lose my cassettes and I lose a friend. Now, every time I see him he sneers at me."

Ginger glanced down at Normie, who appeared to be taking everything in.

Herbie raved on like a man possessed.

"And it's not just your friends, it's companies too!" he shouted; then, as if to confide in Ginger, threw his arm around Ginger's shoulder and whispered, "Take chewing gum wrappers."

"Chewing gum wrappers," echoed Ginger.

"Exactly. I knew a smart feller like you would understand, Meggsie," said Herbie. "Yeah, chewing gum wrappers and the BMX bike they promise you'll win if

76

you collect the whole alphabet. How many times have you bought chewy and checked out the wrapper? I must have done it a zillion times and I've never ever got past 'L'. I don't reckon they ever printed one from A to Z."

Ginger, who had held similar suspicions himself, had to agree but he was still puzzled as to what this had to do with the education of young Normie.

"Well, what's that got to do with your brother?"

"I'm going to teach him not to be a terrible great sucker like I am," answered Herbie.

"Oh!" said Ginger.

"You know the scouts' slogan, 'Be Prepared!', well no one's going to be more prepared than Normie!" boasted Herbie, his hands on his hips.

"Okay, Normie," he continued. "Up that tree."

Little Normie obeyed, robot-like, and scurried up to the first branch of a wattle tree near the pathway.

"Good, Normie. Stand up on the first branch," ordered Herbie.

Again Normie immediately did as he was told.

"Righto, Normie boy, jump and I'll catch you," said Herbie, holding out his arms.

Normie launched himself from the branch.

"That's the boy," shouted Herbie gleefully.

Down came Normie towards the waiting arms of his brother; then, with centimetres left to fall, Herbie jumped aside, matador-like, and, much to Ginger's horror, watched calmly as Normie ploughed into the ground.

Moments passed. Herbie didn't say a word. Ginger

"THAT'S THE BOY."

couldn't. Mike and Tony stood flabbergasted. Normie emerged from the dirt and pile of dead leaves looking numb but with a crooked grin across his little freckled face.

Herbie grinned back and patted his brother's head.

"But . . . but you said you'd catch him," said Ginger, bewildered by what had just happened.

"That's his first great lesson in how not to be a terrible great sucker," said Herbie proudly. "Never trust *anybody* — not even your own brother."

Ginger watched amazed as Herbie and Normie, the former still waving his arms and talking non stop, the latter a little wiser about "terrible great suckers" and how to avoid becoming one, proceeded down the pathway through the park.

"Coming, Ginger?" shouted Herbie. "I've got lots more to teach him. A smart feller like you could help."

"Naw, I don't think I could take the strain," answered Ginger.

"See y' round then," said Herbie.

Ginger shook his head, put his hands in his pockets and strolled on. By the time he'd reached Minnie Peters's, he had almost forgotten the Haeburn brothers and the great lesson in life.

Ginger was about to knock on Min's back door when it suddenly opened.

"Oh!" he said, startled, his fist still going through the knocking motions in midair. He looked up to see an equally startled Mrs Peters staring down at him.

"Good gracious, Ginger," she said. "You frightened

the daylights out of me." Then she called through the door, "Jasmin, you have a visitor."

She shook the table cloth she was holding and let the crumbs fall into the garden.

"I'm afraid you're too late for lunch," she said crisply. Ginger was not one of her favourite people. Just then Minnie came to the door.

"What a lovely surprise, Ginger," she said.

"Don't be too long, Jasmin. Your father's nearly ready," said Mrs Peters, brushing past Ginger.

"Yes, Mother," said Minnie. She turned back to Ginger.

"I'm afraid we've already eaten lunch," she said.

"Gee, Min! What is it about everyone around this place? You'd think a feller only ever came here when he was hungry or something!" grumbled Ginger.

"Of course we don't think that, Ginger," mused Minnie.

"Well, as a matter of fact, I've come around with top news," said Ginger positively. "You'll never guess..."

"You'll never guess..." said Minnie, interrupting Ginger in mid sentence. "Now don't move!" She disappeared inside.

"But...but...oh...Min! The parade! Do you wanner...Oh, what's the use, women never want to listen."

Ginger slumped down on the doorstep and waited.

Minnie returned almost as quickly as she had left.

"Surprise!" she said, holding out a large chocolate-covered cake.

A broad smile came over Ginger's face.

"Unreal!" he said.

"It's my very first cake, Ginger," said Minnie proudly. "Mother let me make it all by myself. It's full of lots of good stuff like nuts and raisins and everything."

Ginger bit his lips in anticipation.

"It was supposed to be banana covered in yellow icing, but I didn't have any so I used a lemon and chocolate instead. I'm going to let you have it."

"Top stuff," muttered Ginger with delight as Minnie handed him the cake.

"Wait till Coogan hears about this," he thought.

"Look, I can't stay and chat because Father's taking Mother and I to an antique auction this afternoon," explained Minnie. "But I'll ring you up later and you can tell me what you think of it."

"IT'S MY VERY FIRST CAKE."

"Gosh, you're marvellous, Min! Gee, thanks. Golly, I bet I'm the luckiest feller ever, I bet," gasped Ginger, overjoyed.

The thought of the parade had gone right out of his mind.

Ginger strutted happily along the street, unaware that his every move was being observed from nearby.

"Boy, Mum won't even worry about that old watermelon when she sees this cake, I bet," he said to Mike and Tony who followed close behind, both obviously hoping for a share of Minnie's handiwork.

Ginger had almost reached the safety of his lane when...

"Well, if it isn't the high-wire walker of the month, Mr Carrot Top Meggs himself." It was Tiger Kelly.

"Er...good day, Tige," squirmed Ginger, hiding the cake behind his back.

"There's a certain matter of a wet, slimy watermelon skin I want to discuss with you, man to microbe."

"Just a joke, Tige...you know...a laugh?"

"I'm not laughing, Meggsie, or hadn't you noticed?" said Tiger bluntly.

He grabbed Ginger by the arm.

"Ow!" winced Ginger.

Then Tiger spotted the cake.

"What have you got there?" he asked.

"Nothing you'd want, Tige." Ginger felt his arm being squeezed very hard. "Just a sort of cake, Tige," he added.

"Give us it 'ere," said Kelly roughly, snatching the

cake. "Just what I feel like, and m' favourite, too!"

Kelly broke a large chunk off the side and began eating it. Ginger watched morosely as, bit by bit, Tiger devoured it — sucking in one chunk after another, until all that remained was a small pyramid of crumbs on the ground between his boots.

"You're doing the right thing, Meggsie," mumbled Kelly, his mouth full to overflowing. "Keep giving me cakes like this and you won't get hurt," he added as he sucked the chocolate icing off his thumbs and fingers. "Not as much, anyway." He laughed. "Now, as to the little matter of the. . ."

Kelly's face suddenly went green, his cheeks puffed out, making him look like a lovesick frog, and he grabbed his stomach with both hands.

"Argh!" he screamed, and doubled over in pain. His legs shot straight out in front of him then bent up to his chest.

His face went a dark shade of blue, then yellow, but, before it had time to work its way through the entire rainbow spectrum, he fell with a loud thud to the ground, gasping for breath and rolling over and over, like an empty drink can down a hill.

"Argh!" he screamed again. "Oh, oh, my stomach! I'm poisoned. Get me to a doctor, quick. Argh!"

Ginger looked around; the street was unusually deserted. He glanced back at Kelly lying in agony, still clutching his stomach. He had to do something — but what? There was no way he could carry someone that heavy to the doctor's.

Tony tugged at Ginger's shorts and pointed across the road. There was someone with a wheelbarrow in the park.

"Good boy, Tony," said Ginge. "That'll do the trick."

Ginger was in such a rush that he was at the other side of the street when he discovered that the wheelbarrow was being pushed by none other than Eddie Coogan paying his debt to Darky Nolan, who sat in the front grinning with fear at Ginger's approach.

"What do you want, Meggs?" asked Coogan scornfully.

"Your wheelbarrow," answered Ginger.

"Yeah and pigs might fly, too."

"Look, Coogan, there isn't time to argue. Tiger Kelly's over there — dying I reckon, and you've got to take him to the doctor's."

"You're out of your brain, Meggs," said Coogan.

"Am I! What if when he recovers Tiger finds out who wouldn't take him to the doctor? What then, eh?" said Ginger. "Who do you think he'll take apart bit by bit?"

Coogan thought for a moment, then roughly emptied Darky out onto the footpath.

"Where is he?" he asked bitterly.

Ginger pointed to Kelly.

Coogan grudgingly crossed the road, mumbling and cursing as he did.

Ginger looked down to see Darky Nolan still on the ground where he'd been emptied. "Just a bit of advice, mate," he said. "If I were you I'd be over there helping Coogan load Tige into the wheelbarrow, then I'd be

helping to take him to the doctor's. Get it?"

"Yes, Ginge, whatever you say," spluttered Darky as he made a beeline to where Coogan was struggling with the groaning Kelly.

Ginger watched contentedly as Coogan and Darky did their best to wheel the writhing patient to Dr Russell's. He estimated that Tiger had fallen out of the wheelbarrow at least thirteen times in the first one hundred metres; at that rate he'd have to be treated for severe bruising as well as food poisoning.

"What a day," grinned Ginger and then, remembering the terrible gluttony with which Tiger Kelly had sucked up every crumb of cake and scrape of icing, he laughed out loud.

"What he needs, boys," he said to Mike and Tony, "what would really benefit Mister Kelly, is a lesson from Herbie Haeburn on how to overcome his tendency towards being one of the world's truly deaf-defying, terrible great suckers."

Chapter 6
The Art Treasure

JOHN Meggs was having one of those days. It was one thing after another. The phone hadn't stopped from the moment he'd arrived at the office. The continual "BR...ring, BR...ring" had given him a gigantic headache that not even aspirins could relieve. To make matters worse, he was suffering from a mild attack of indigestion, caused by having to gobble down his lunch while trying to cope with an influx of extra work.

Orders that were supposed to go out, *hadn't*. Others that weren't, *had*. A mountain range of papers lay in peaks across his desk and was growing higher by the minute. He'd spilt coffee in his lap, stapled his tie to an urgent batch of mail, destroyed his expensive fountain pen when he accidentally put it in the pencil sharpener, and had been reprimanded by his boss for being overly liberal with paper clips. If all that wasn't bad enough for one day, he had had to put up with the incessant boasting and gabbling of Jake Glutz with whom he unfortunately had to share the shoebox that the Company called the "dispatch office"!

Somehow Glutz always managed to finish his work early and spend a good part of the day sitting on the edge of Meggs's desk expounding the attributes and virtues of his son, Joseph, with whom Ginger attended the local public school.

"Yes, Meggs, my boy is a wonderful scholar. Breezes through his exams. Top of his class last year," boasted Glutz.

"So you keep telling me," said Mr Meggs, endeavouring to get on with his work.

"Your boy Ginger could do a lot worse than take after him," continued Glutz.

"You keep telling me that, too. And as I keep telling you, Sarah and I are more than happy with Ginger's progress," said Mr Meggs.

That was an out-and-out lie since Ginger had had the distinction of coming last in class for the past four years. Somehow, though, he'd managed to scrape through every year. Mr and Mrs Meggs, although always surprised, were also always thankful.

"My young Joseph will probably end up being a famous brain surgeon, I shouldn't doubt," bragged Glutz.

"Great," muttered Mr Meggs under his breath. "Maybe he'll be able to do something with *your* brain."

"What did y' say, Meggs?" enquired Glutz, who had been far more concerned with hearing himself talk than

"SO YOU KEEP TELLING ME."

listening to anything John Meggs might have to say.

"Um...er...um," stuttered Mr Meggs, embarrassed. "Um...almost time to get the train," he said, looking at his watch.

"So it is, so it is. Time sure gets away from you when you're having fun," laughed Glutz loudly, as he was often prone to do.

"Yeah," agreed Mr Meggs reluctantly, trying hard to raise a smile.

Glutz grabbed Mr Meggs's coat and bowler hat from the stand.

"Catch!" he said, lobbing them at him.

Mr Meggs made a furious but futile attempt to snatch the coat and hat as they sailed over his head, and in doing so upset a full bottle of liquid paper over a particularly long invoice he had almost finished.

"Cripes!" he said despondently, then looked around in time to see his apparel land in the used coffee-cup bin.

"Ah, you'll never make the cricket team," bellowed Glutz. "Are you coming?"

Mr Meggs fumed. It was all he could do to stop himself exploding. He took a deep breath, then smiled politely through clenched teeth. The last thing he wanted to do was sit in a train next to Glutz and listen to further instalments about "wonderful young Joseph" all the way home.

"No, as a matter of fact, I won't be taking the train," he said. "Thought I'd walk home for a change."

"Oh, well, suit yourself. See you tomorrow."

"Unfortunately, yes," said Mr Meggs under his breath.

"What was that?" asked Glutz as he was leaving the room.

"Er, look forward to it; yes," Mr Meggs coughed.

He looked at the mountains on his desk and the mess surrounding them. Had he the energy, he could scream.

"Come to think of it, I could do with a walk," he said to himself.

"Auction Sale — Now On — Step Inside" read the sign propped up against the shop window.

"Hm!" pondered Mr Meggs. "I might pick up a bargain."

He strolled in and stood at the back of the room. The auctioneer, a round little man with a yellow moustache

and balding head, stood on an empty soft-drink crate and addressed the large crowd through an old, rusty microphone.

"Now then, ladies an' gents, whad am I offered for this...this... combination clock and priceless work of art?" He held up a large plastic statue, a rendering of Michelangelo's *David* with a digital contraption in its navel.

"Looks like the artist had an attack of bad taste," thought Mr Meggs.

Hands began shooting up all around him. The auctioneer started spraying out numbers and, as the figures rose, so did the colour of his nose.

"Ten, do I have twelve? Yes fifteen! Twenty — five, thirty — five — forty." His nose was now quite cherry red. "Any advance on forty? Goin' once, goin'. Sold," he shouted, and banged his hammer down loudly. "The man in the green shirt. Our next lot is..."

"The things some people buy!" said Mr Meggs, shaking his head in disgust. "They must have more money than sense."

"...is this lovely, fully framed masterpiece. You can still read the numbers through the paint. Right, who's going to start me off?"

This time only a couple of hands shot up.

"Five," shouted the roly-poly. Mr Meggs decided that the painting was the last thing he would want hanging in his house and his eyes began to wander around the room. Standing in the corner he noticed Mr and Mrs Peters and Minnie.

"Peters," he called in a half whisper that failed to attract their attention. He edged closer.

"Ten..." The bidding was hardly brisk enough to turn the auctioneer's nose to pink.

"Peters," Mr Meggs called, a little louder, again with no response.

He pushed his way through the crowd and waved.

"...fifteen..." shouted the auctioneer.

"Peters," called Mr Meggs, but still he failed to catch the Peterses' attention.

Mr Meggs waved again.

"...twenty, I have twenty!" blasted through the speaker system. "Am I offered any more? Once, twice, three times."

Bang! went the hammer.

"Sold to the gent in the bowler hat."

With a final shove Mr Meggs made his way up to the Peterses.

"'Afternoon all," he said, greeting the Peterses with a wry smile. "I wonder what fool got lumbered with that piece of junk?"

They stared at him, wide-eyed. "Why, I think you did, Mr Meggs," said Mrs Peters.

A large man in a pair of grubby, faded overalls tapped Mr Meggs on the shoulder. "That's twenty bucks, thanks, pal," he said in a gruff tone.

"Well done, John," said Mr Peters. "Always said you had an eye for art." He tried to hold back a smile.

"But — I — but," stammered Mr Meggs.

"Twenty bucks — cash," said the man in the overalls.

"Now look here..."

"Listen, mister, you bid for it and you're going to pay for it and you're going to take it away, or would you prefer me to call an ambulance for you?" he said in a nasty way.

Mr Meggs ambled along the footpath.

"Dreadful people. Blackguards, that's what they are," said Mr Meggs to himself as he walked on home with his painting tucked under his arm. "I should go straight to the police," he grumbled. "A bloke should have gone home on the train. It's all Glutz's fault. Wait till I tell Sarah."

He stopped dead in his tracks.

"What *am* I going to tell Sarah!"

"BLACKGUARDS, THAT'S WHAT THEY ARE."

"But, Mum," pleaded Ginger in earnest. "It was an accident. Honest it was!"

Sarah Meggs stood with her arms folded and eyes narrowed. Her foot tapped impatiently on the linoleum floor.

"So it was an accident!" She raised one eyebrow and looked down suspiciously at her chattering son.

Ginger thought for a moment.

"Well, Mum, you could call it that. Gee, I didn't bump into Bader on purpose," he said with his eyes downcast. "If I'd known it was our watermelon...I mean, you know how much I like watermelon."

"And I know how much watermelons cost," replied Mrs Meggs sternly.

Ginger knew he was losing ground rapidly and needed to tackle the problem from another direction.

"The reason I was running, Mum, was because," he lowered his tone as if to indicate he had decided to come clean and confide in her, "I was chasing this kid, see."

"Oh, a nanny goat or a billy goat?" asked Mrs Meggs.

"No, not that kind of a kid, a feller — Darky Nolan, actually." Ginger smiled, pleased with his sudden rush of inspiration and hoping to get a more positive reaction from his mother.

Mrs Meggs remained stonefaced. Ginger continued.

"I was chasing him because he said his mother was better than mine. Well, he didn't say it, but I knew that's what he was thinking."

"I see! Now you're a mind-reader," said Mrs Meggs, trying to hold back a smile.

Ginger was quick to pick up the subtle change in his mother's tone. This was the opportunity he needed.

"Let's not talk of that, Mum!" he said, almost patronisingly. "Any feller who thinks his mother is better than mine is halfway to the hospital."

"Oh, you're proud of your mother?"

"Who wouldn't be proud of a good-looking, understanding woman with a heart of gold and who's terrible good to her children?"

Ginger hopped up on a kitchen chair, brushed his hair out of his eyes, put one hand, Napoleon like, into his vest and raised the other high into the air.

"A woman who would stand by her son against the world," he intoned. "A terrible respectable woman who would DIE for her own flesh and blood."

He paused, as if awaiting a sound of applause, closed his eyes and pointed to his mother. In his mind the

"... WITH A HEART OF GOLD..."

96

orchestra had reached a climax and flowers were raining on to the stage. Ginger smiled, and opened his eyes optimistically.

Mrs Meggs was unmoved. Ginger's smile faded. There was an anguished pause, then Mrs Meggs spoke quietly but deliberately.

"This wonderful woman is — I take it — the same one that happened to be told by a little birdie — who shall remain nameless..." she raised her voice a fraction, "...that you were skylarking around and bumped into young Teddy Bader on purpose!" She grabbed Ginger by the ear.

Ginger was taken aback.

"Huh?" was the only response that came to his lips.

"Get up to your room and wait for your father! It's about time you learnt the value of money and respect for other people. Try telling your father about gold hearts."

Ginger sat forlornly on the edge of his bed. He looked at Mike and Tony and shrugged dejectedly.

"I must be losing my touch. Slipping! In the old days Mum would be turning away and wiping her eyes," he said pathetically, then lay down to await his father's arrival.

"Sarah, I'm home," shouted Mr Meggs as he closed the front door behind him.

"In the kitchen," answered Mrs Meggs.

Mr Meggs hung up his coat and bowler then continued on gingerly to the kitchen with the newly acquired piece of art. His wife was putting the finishing touches to the evening meal.

"I was beginning to get a little worried," she said. "I've already fed Dudley and put him to bed."

"I decided to walk home instead of getting the train. Ended up bumping into the Peterses."

Mr Meggs walked into the kitchen holding up the painting in front of his face. Mrs Meggs, unaware of what was happening behind her back, began dishing out the vegetables.

"Sit down, dinner's just about ready," she said. "Oh, give Ginger a call, will you. I had to send him to his room. I want you to deal with him . . ."

She turned around to see Mr Meggs peering around from the back of the painting.

"What on earth is that?" Mrs Meggs exclaimed loudly, nearly dropping the dinner plates on the floor.

"A little surprise, Sarah. Something to brighten up the lounge room. If I'm any judge of art, it's worth a lot of money," said Mr Meggs, as convincingly as his conscience would allow.

"Good heavens, John," retorted Mrs Meggs.

"I admit it's a little bright but it's what the room needs," continued Mr Meggs. "And, for only twenty dollars . . ."

"Twenty dollars? *Twenty dollars!*" boomed Mrs Meggs.

"*Only* twenty dollars. A real bargain!" countered Mr Meggs.

"And I thought your son had no idea about money."

Ginger, who had heard the commotion, popped his head around the door.

"You called, Mum? Gee, Dad, where'd y' get the unreal picture!" he said.

"Ah, there, Ginger, run along and get me a hammer and nail," Mr Meggs commanded.

Ginger raced out to the shed.

"Don't tell me you're actually going to hang that in the house?" enquired Mrs Meggs, not really believing that her husband would even contemplate such an act.

"And why not? I intend to get my full twenty dollars' worth out of it," said Mr Meggs.

Mrs Meggs shook her head in disbelief.

"What was it you wanted me to talk to Ginger about?" asked Mr Meggs, trying to change the conversation.

"It doesn't matter any more, I'm not sure he'd believe you anyway," said Mrs Meggs.

Ginger returned with the necessary tools.

"Above the fireplace should suit it," said Mr Meggs.

"In the fireplace would be more like it," quipped Mrs Meggs.

John Meggs ignored his wife's sarcasm and set about hanging the painting.

"Get me that chair please, Ginger," he said.

He didn't like the painting any more than she did but had decided on the way home that no matter what he did he was going to be nagged at for the next couple of days at least; if that was the case he preferred to be accused of lack of artistic taste rather than hounded for being a wastrel.

"There, how's that?" he asked.

"Dinner's probably cold by now," said Mrs Meggs,

returning to the kitchen.

"Well, Ginger?"

"I think it needs to go a bit to the right, Dad."

Mr Meggs adjusted the painting.

"A bit more, I reckon. That's just about it," said Ginger.

The painting was almost straight when, for no apparent reason, one of the legs of the chair snapped.

Mr Meggs grabbed at the wall, but got the painting instead. "Oops! Argh!" he cried as he crashed to the ground.

Crunch!

Mrs Meggs, who could not help but hear the noise, came running back and surveyed the damage. There, in the middle of the floor, sat her husband, covered in pieces of broken plaster with his head through the middle of what used to be the painting.

Ginger and Mrs Meggs tried hard not to laugh. Mr Meggs saw nothing funny in it at all. Not only was his pride hurt but his head and backside were both suffering as well.

"Don't just stand there," he shouted, "give me a hand."

Ginger carefully lifted the frame off his father's head, As he did, two fifty-dollar notes floated out from the back of the painting.

"Dad, look at the money that's come out of the picture," said Ginger excitedly. "Two fifty-buck notes! Wow."

Mrs Meggs could not believe her eyes.

TWO FIFTY-DOLLAR NOTES

"Great Scot!" said Mr Meggs. "Evidently hidden there years ago and forgotten."

"One hundred dollars!" said Mrs Meggs, taking it out of her husband's hands and putting it into her apron pocket. "That will just about cover the cost of your precious piece of art, the chair you so expertly demolished and the plaster and paint to repair the wall," she said. "It might also just pay for the watermelon."

"Told you it would be worth big money one day," smiled Mr Meggs.

"Yes, John. Perhaps you are a good judge of art. Even if it did have to hit *you* over the head before *I* realised it," said Mrs Meggs. "Dinner's on," she added smartly.

Mr Meggs looked at Ginger proudly, as if to say, "I hope you learnt something out of all that." Then something occurred to him.

"Plaster, paint, chair," he mumbled to himself, "watermelon?"

What on earth did Sarah say that for?

"What's all this about watermelon?" he asked with a puzzled frown.

Mrs Meggs winked at her son. "Nothing, just watermelon," she said.

Ginger grinned from ear to ear!

Chapter 7
A Friend in Need

"IT was t'rific to the enth degree, Bennie," said Ginger enthusiastically as the pair wandered down the street, heading nowhere in particular and taking their time getting there.

"It was fantastic! Unbelievably fan-ripper-tastic! You should have been there."

"Wo-ow," responded Bennie slowly, shaking his head in awe at the very thought.

"There was Tige, rolling and moaning and as helpless as a wounded prawn in a flock of starving seagulls, while smarmy ol' Coogan and his weak-kneed mate Nolan kept accidentally tipping him out of the wheelbarrow onto the footpath all the way down the street."

"Ex-cell-ent stuff!" smiled Bennie. "What I wouldn't have given to see that!"

"The best bit, but. . ." continued Ginger, trying to control himself long enough to finish his story, ". . . was the way Tige, as sick as he was, was still threatening to bash them, in between groans."

The two boys doubled up with laughter and it was nearly two blocks before Ginger was able to gather his wits and talk again.

"The doctor reckons he'll be all right soon," he said, as seriously as the moment allowed. "What worries me is Min. It'd break her heart if she knew her cake was no good."

"Easy," advised Bennie. "Don't tell her."

"She'll want to know what I thought of it," replied Ginger.

"Well, just tell her Tiger Kelly nicked it off you and leave it at that. She'll understand."

"Yeah, you're right," said Ginger thoughtfully.

"Course I am," Bennie assured him. "If there's one thing I know all about, it's women."

"Don't let me forget to ask Min to go to the Australia Day parade and show with me," said Ginger. "If I don't ask her soon it'll be too late."

His brow darkened. His tone deepened. "I wouldn't put it past a creep like Coogan to ask her himself, just to get even with a feller," he said intensely.

Bennie's sympathetic look was evidence that he agreed with Ginger.

"No worries," he said staunchly, giving his mate the thumbs-up sign.

Ginger and Bennie decided that a morning spent sitting around on their favourite corner, and thereby running the risk of being shouted a shake or a sundae, was as good a way as any to pass the time.

As the boys approached the corner they noticed that it

was already occupied. On closer inspection it fortunately proved to be little Hookey Hooks who was sitting there with his poodle pup, Sergeant Peppers, or Pepe, as everyone called him.

That was a relief. To use "Meggsie's Spot", as it was known in certain circles, without a prior invitation from Ginger himself, was tantamount to walking under a ladder with a black cat on Friday the thirteenth. It was rarely done, but occasionally a smart alec new kid, or a weed trying to make a name for himself, would put the edict to the test. To date no one had ever dared twice.

Hookey Hooks was one of those few lucky people allowed to use "Meggsie's Spot" without having to ask first.

"Ah, there, Hookey," said Ginger cheerily. "There y' go Pepe."

"Hello, Ginger," said Hookey softly, with the faintest trace of a tear in his eye.

Hookey Hooks held a special place in Ginger's gang. Although a couple of years younger than the others, he was in no way subordinate. A quietly spoken but tough little guy, time and time again he had stood up for Ginger and the others and more often than not had suffered a bleeding nose or a black eye for his trouble.

Hookey could be relied on to be there whenever the going got tough. When it came to loyalty he was never found wanting. As far as Hookey was concerned, Ginger Meggs was boss and could do no wrong. His special thing in the whole world was the photo of Ginger and himself that hung in pride of place above his bed. It was taken

the day they had managed to put on a match-saving,
tenth-wicket partnership of fifty-two runs, against an all-
out speed onslaught by the rough and tough Bystanders
team.

It was Ginger who had scored fifty of the winning
runs, but it was "Stonewall" Hookey who had weathered a
vicious, intimidatory bumper storm and stayed there,
despite being painfully felled on three separate occasions.

"What's up, big feller?" asked Ginger, genuinely
concerned.

A moment passed before Hookey spoke.

"I've got to go up to the public library and tell them
about that book," he said. "An' I'm scared of what they
might do to me."

"Is that all? No worries," said Ginger, lifting Hookey to his feet. "I'll go with you."

"Me too," said Bennie.

"In fact, we'll all go. Mike, Tony, Pepe, the lot of us. What do you say to that?" asked Ginger.

"Gee, would you, Ginge?" exclaimed Hookey.

The public library was a musty old building full of dark, wood-panelled corridors that seemed to go on for ever, and hundreds of marble statues of people's heads that appeared to be there solely to keep guard over the books. It was run by an equally musty old librarian called Mr Searle, who had the reputation of hating kids and taking great delight in demanding their pocket money to pay for any damaged or overdue books.

Ginger had never had much call to use the library. He reasoned that any place that wouldn't let a feller talk or run around, if he so desired, and that charged money to use the toilets, was better left to sissies like the Cuthbert Fitzcloons of this world.

The only recent occasion he had visited the library was on a school excursion. On that occasion Mr Searle had escorted him out, nose first, when he was caught playing marbles for money in the Greek Mythology section.

"There it is!" said Ginger, pointing to a sign painted on the glass panel of a door, that read:

"MR W. SEARLE. B.A., T.S.M., A.N.
HEAD LIBRARIAN
KNOCK (VERY QUIETLY) BEFORE ENTERING"

Ginger puffed his chest out as far as he was able. "Now remember," he said to Hookey, "let me do all the talking."

He knocked on the door.

"You may come in," said Mr Searle, almost regally, and only just loudly enough to be heard.

"Oh, it's you, Meggs," he grimaced. "And what may we do for you?"

Ginger strutted forward confidently while Hookey and Bennie cautiously remained near the doorway.

"I've come to tell you that Mr Hooks here . . ." Ginger pointed to Hookey, who reluctantly took a small pace forward, ". . . has lost a book he borrowed."

Ginger folded his arms resolutely, almost daring Mr Searle to speak.

Mr Searle slowly removed the pince-nez he had sitting on the end of his bulbous nose, squinted his eyes and spoke in a very matter-of-fact tone of voice.

"In that case, Master Hooks will have to pay for the book. Fifteen dollars is the standing charge, I believe."

Hookey blanched at the mention of the two-figure sum.

Ginger, noticing this, shook his head and gave Hookey a reassuring glance. He'd fight fire with fire. He squinted his eyes and leant with both hands on the front of Mr Searle's book-covered desk.

"How can you ask a feller with no money to pay for a book?" He raised his voice, "How can you do it?" He deliberated, then spoke quietly, "How?" The last query was delivered in a dramatically hushed tone.

"HOW CAN YOU DO IT ?"

Mr Searle was unmoved. He stood up and peered down at Ginger.

"How? Rules! I'm sorry, but those are the rules. I have to abide by the rules, Master Hooks has to abide by the rules, and even you, Master Meggs, should the occasion ever arise, and hopefully it never will, you too will have to abide by the rules!"

Ginger was not about to be put off. Rules after all were only there to be broken. He dragged Hookey forward, nearly causing him to trip on the mat in front of Mr Searle's desk. The stumble added impetus to his argument.

"Can you get blood out of a stone? Look at him! A poor, hungry, starving feller that can hardly stand on his own two feet. A skeleton. . .with a heart of *gold!*"

Mr Searle was dumbfounded at the intensity of Ginger's speech.

"Do you want this delicate feller," continued Ginger, "to go home and be beaten, maybe unconscious, for losing a mingy old book? Do you want that on your conscience?"

"Dear me, now, dear, oh dear," stammered Mr Searle, obviously distressed by the verbal bombardment. "Tch, tch, dear me."

Ginger could sense victory.

"A million books here, but no!" he shouted. "Hound a feller! Call out the police! The army! ASIO! And have him shot down. . ."

"Now, now, Meggs," said Mr Searle, "will you kindly keep your voice down. *Please*!" he shouted. "Never mind about the book. Forget it. Just get out of my office! All of you, out of my office."

He watched, relieved, as Ginger led his small party out into the corridor.

"Tch, tch," he sighed, rolling his eyes to the ceiling. Exhausted, he slumped into his chair.

"Thanks, Ginger, you were marvellous," said Hookey gratefully when they were once again on their home patch.

"Wait till I tell Mum, she'll be rapt. Carn, Pepe. See you."

Hookey ran excitedly down the back lane that led home. Ginger and Bennie watched as he disappeared through a hole in the back fence.

"Ginge," said Bennie after a moment, "I wonder how young Hookey's book got lost?"

"He lent it to me," said Ginger softly as he pushed his back gate open.

"HE LENT IT TO ME."

Chapter 8
A Helping Hand

"**S**O you've finally decided to come home, then?" said Mrs Meggs as she struggled past the wire door with a large basket full of wet washing.

"Before you do another thing, young man, go inside and phone Minnie Peters. She has been calling all morning. Something about a cake. She said you'd know what she was talking about."

"Won't be a sec, Bennie," said Ginger, racing inside.

"Don't bang that..."

The wire door slammed loudly behind Ginger.

"...wire door! I sometimes wonder if I raised a son or a cheer squad," said Mrs Meggs.

Bennie looked up and smiled politely.

"Can I help you with the pegs, Mrs M?" he asked.

"That'd be nice," replied Mrs Meggs.

The washing was just about hung out when Ginger finally returned from the house. He was deep in thought and for the first time in living memory closed the wire door quietly behind him.

Mrs Meggs stared disbelievingly as Ginger floated past, unaware of anything around him.

She shook her head and went inside.

"Gee, you took a long time, Ginge," said Bennie.

He failed to get a reaction from his red-headed mate.

"It must have been a real good talk," he said, a little louder.

Ginger snapped back to the present. "Er, sorry, Bennie," he said.

"You were ages."

"You know how females are on the phone," said Ginger apologetically.

"Too right!" said Bennie knowingly. "My dad reckons Mum ought to move into the local phone box, she spends so much time in there anyway."

"What does your mum say to him?"

"She never hears him. She's always too busy talking."

"Oh," said Ginger dryly.

"How did you go, then?" asked Bennie.

"Go?" Ginger looked blank.

"About Tiger and the cake."

"Oh that," replied Ginger. "I did like you said. I told Min that Tige nicked it from me and ate it. She said not to worry, she'd make me another one and I could eat it all at her place."

They both slumped to the ground against the fence.

"That's a bit of bad luck, Ginge."

"Maybe she won't get time," said Ginger. "A guy can hope, I s'pose."

Ginger and Bennie sat in silence, staring up at the clouds. There didn't seem anything worth saying, so no one said anything.

Mike and Tony chased each other around the yard.

After a short while Bennie remembered. "Did you ask her to go to the parade?" he enquired.

"Not really; well no, not at all. I didn't exactly get a chance."

"What did y' talk about?" asked Bennie, reluctantly, not wanting to sound like a busybody, but eager to know.

"Aggie Hopkins's charm bracelet. Min wants to buy one," said Ginger.

"Typical woman," nodded Bennie authoritatively.

"They cost twelve dollars and she's only got three dollars. She's a bit down 'cause Aggie keeps showing off. I wish I could give her a helping hand," sighed Ginger.

"Why don't you just break into your moneybox and give her the money?" suggested Bennie.

Ginger shook his head slowly from side to side.

"I don't reckon there's that much in my moneybox and I'm not sure I can break into it. Dad made certain he got me a 'Ginger-proof' one this time. Anyway," he concluded, "I was going to break into it to get the money to buy the Australia Day show tickets."

"That's still a week off, Ginge. If you did odd jobs and messages you could raise that much by then," advised Bennie.

"Even if I did have the money," countered Ginger,

"Min wouldn't accept it. She's terrible proud like that. She'd be insulted, I reckon. I could never think of giving her money."

Bennie suddenly sprang to his feet.

"I've got a great idea, Ginge! Listen. What about going up to Min and saying, 'I can get you one of those charm bracelets, just like Aggie's and it will only cost three dollars!'" he beamed.

Ginger was confused. "Where would I get a twelve-dollar charm bracelet for three dollars?" he asked.

"That's just it," continued Bennie. "You can't."

"What's the point?" asked Ginger.

"She gives you her three dollars. You put in nine bucks and Min gets her bracelet, and she need never know the truth."

Ginger was impressed. Very impressed.

"Golly! What a beaut idea," he said. "Let's check out my 'Ginger-proof' moneybox. I'll get the hammer."

Ginger sat on the end of his bed sorting out a pile of coins. His moneybox lay shattered on the floor. "Four dollars in notes. Two in fifty cent pieces makes six. One dollar in twenty cents, a dollar and ten in tens, forty cents worth of shrapnel including a New Zealand five cents. What's that?"

Bennie hesitated a minute, then answered, "Eight fifty."

"Fifty cents short! Wouldn't it rot y'," said Ginger, looking dejectedly at Bennie.

Mike whimpered in sympathy. Tony did a back somersault then dived under the bed. Moments later he

popped up with a dusty fifty-cent piece and dropped it in Ginger's lap.

"How the...? Where the...?"

"You beauty!" said Ginger and Bennie in unison.

"Here's my three dollars, Ginge," said Minnie hesitantly. "But are you sure you can get a charm bracelet so cheaply?"

Ginger smiled broadly with a twinkle in his eyes.

"No worries, Min," he said. "I'll get it for you, but I can't tell you where on account it's a terrible top secret. I won't be long."

Ginger didn't waste any time getting down to Hasham's jewellery shop in the main street.

"That one there, please," he puffed.

"A charm bracelet," said Mr Hasham. "That will cost you twelve dollars, son."

"That's the very exactly money I've got in my hand ready, mister," said Ginger, pleased with himself. "Golly, is this going to make Min happy!"

Ginger returned to the Peterses' home in record time.

"Oh, Ginger! This is *lovely* — and it only cost three dollars! Wait till Aggie Hopkins sees it," giggled Minnie.

She leant forward and kissed Ginger on the cheek.

"Thank you very much, Ginger. You're too sweet!"

Ginger's face turned almost as red as his hair. Even his freckles seemed to blend in. He was tongue-tied as he tried to speak.

"I've g...g...got to go, M...Min," he stammered. "I've got to meet Bennie down the street."

But he soon regained his composure, and said, "We're going to try and get some odd jobs to raise money for a special event. I can't tell you what it is just yet but. See y' round."

Bennie was standing in front of Joe's milk bar when he saw Ginger, Mike and Tony running towards him. He could tell by the happy look on Ginger's face that their little plan had been successful. Before he had a chance to ask, Ginger was telling him all about it.

"Gee, Bennie, it worked *beautifully*," said Ginger, excitedly. "I picked up the bracelet from Hasham's, then went straight back to Min's. I said it only cost three dollars and she thought that's what I paid for it. Boy, was she happy!"

"She certainly looks happy enough," said Bennie, glancing over Ginger's shoulder. "Here she is now."

"Er...hi, Min," said Ginger, surprised.

"I'm glad I found you," said Minnie. "After you left I got thinking about what you said about having to raise

"OH, GINGER! THIS IS LOVELY."

money for a special event."

Minnie could see Ginger was confused.

"Well, you were so kind getting me that charm bracelet," she continued, "that I worked out a way to make money for you."

Ginger and Bennie looked at each other, then back to Min, not sure what to expect.

"I sold the charm bracelet to Meagan King's mother next door, for five dollars, so..." Minnie opened her purse, "here's your two dollars profit and my three dollars so you can get me another one."

Ginger went numb all over.

"You know," continued Minnie, "if I can keep selling them you could make a fortune." And she smiled sweetly.

Ginger was still numb two hours later.

"Look at it this way, Ginge," said Bennie philosophically. "You got two bucks back and Min believed me when I said our contact had no more bracelets."

Ginger sat motionless. Bennie went on, "Things didn't turn out too bad. As my dad always says, no matter how bad things are they could always be worse."

A pair of great hairy hands grabbed Ginger and Bennie from behind and spun them around.

"Oh no, not you, Tiger! Not now!" moaned Ginger.

Tiger Kelly snarled vengefully. Doom was imminent.

Ginger turned to Bennie. "Your dad got any more great sayings I ought to know?" he croaked.

Chapter 9
The Businessmen

THERE were only two days to go before the Australia Day parade and Ginger was still four dollars fifty short of the money he needed to be able to take Minnie Peters to the gala show at the Town Hall.

Raising the money had proved a little more difficult than either he or Bennie had thought it would be. It had not been helped by the black eye Tiger had inflicted. People didn't feel inclined to trust a feller displaying anything so sporty.

To be on the safe side, Ginger decided not to ask Minnie until the last possible minute. Not that he had given up hope of making his target, but as he had explained to Chubb, it was "just to be on the safe side and to save a feller any unnecessary embarrassment".

"Anyway," he reassured himself, "it'll be more of a surprise that way."

After a week of sweat and yet more bruises, but very little else to show, Bennie had come up with a scheme he guaranteed would make the rest of the cash Ginger needed plus enough for himself as well.

"Home-made lemonade," he said enthusiastically. "This time of year it can't fail. People always want a good, cold drink."

Ginger was a little sceptical. He didn't have the time to waste on something that wasn't a sure-fire hit.

"Well," he pondered for a moment, "I don't know."

"It can't fail, Ginger," said Bennie. "We can get all the lemons we need from Mrs Perry for free. She's got stacks she's always chucking out. We've got enough money to get some sugar and we can get..."

"Water from here in the yard," said Ginger, joining in Bennie's enthusiasm for the scheme. "It'll sure beat having to look after that earache Glennie Sargent again," he said, recalling a disastrous venture from earlier in the

"HOME-MADE LEMONADE,"
SAID BENNIE.

week. "I told y' how he squirted me all over with a water pistol full of ink?"

Bennie nodded.

"For a dollar an hour I can do anything, even baby-sit, but that little feller...flesh and blood can only take just so much," said Ginger gravely.

As the boys had hoped, Mrs Perry loaded them up with all the lemons they could carry.

"You might as well take them. They'll just rot on the ground otherwise," she said.

Ginger bought a kilogram of sugar from the supermarket while Bennie raced back to his place and got his mum's super large plastic bucket.

Tony, and Ginger's young brother, Dudley, helped squeeze the lemons; Bennie poured in the sugar and

stirred while Ginger filled the bucket with water from the back yard tap, using his dad's hose.

"Golly, Ginge, we'll make a nice profit from this lemonade," said Bennie. "We can charge fifty cents a glass for it."

"I reckon we'll get twenty-four glasses out of it," smiled Ginger. "That's twelve dollars. Six each. Enough for me to take Minnie to the show and for you to go as well."

"And a bit left over, for lollies," added Bennie gleefully.

Each of the workers had a free sample of the lemonade in return for their efforts, and in order to check that it tasted okay.

"First thing, Ginge," said Bennie, "we've got to make

an agreement. From now on if either of us wants a drink, we've got to pay for it."

"Certainly. That's only business. In this we've *got* to be businessmen," agreed Ginger.

It was decided that the best place to sell the lemonade would be in the park, on top of Welby Hill.

"By the time people make it up there in this heat," reasoned Ginger, "they'll be dyin' for something to drink."

"Gee, it's heavy," said Bennie, trying to lift the bucket. "No worries," said Ginger, grabbing the old straw broom from behind the wire door and putting it through the handle of the bucket. "With one either side we can both carry it at the same time."

By the time Ginger and Bennie had made the old wrought-iron gates at the entrance to the park, both were puffing and panting.

"Boy, it's hot," said Bennie. "I think I'll have a glass, Ginge."

He dug into his pocket and pulled out a fifty-cent piece.

"Here's my money."

"Hand it over, then," said Ginger, in a businesslike way.

"Gee, she tastes good," said Bennie, downing the lemonade.

"Does she, Bennie? Well I think *I'll* have a glass too," said Ginger. "Here's my fifty cents."

Ginge handed the fifty cents back to Bennie.

"BOY, IT'S HOT!"

Refreshed, they continued through the park towards Welby Hill, struggling under the weight of the bucket and the midday heat.

"Do you know something, Ginge?" said Bennie. "If we were to have another drink the bucket wouldn't be so heavy."

"You're not wrong," replied Ginger. "Give me fifty cents and you go first."

Bennie handed Ginger his money and filled up the glass.

"Top stuff," he said, as the lemonade quickly vanished. "Okay, your turn. Hand over the cash."

Once again the fifty-cent piece changed hands and a glass of lemonade disappeared.

"TOP STUFF!"

Ginger and Bennie reached the bottom of Welby Hill and gazed, exhausted, towards the top.

"Phew," said Ginger, "that's some climb."

"I think I'll need another drink before we start up there," said Bennie.

"Okay, so long as you pay me first," responded Ginger. Then he added, "Seeing we've stopped, Bennie, I'd better buy another one while I'm here."

"Right. Money please."

They drank another glass each, duly paid for it and set off for the crest of the hill.

Ginger squinted up into the sun.

"Golly, she's hot work, Bennie," he panted, the sweat running down his freckles.

"Yes and I bet it's dangerous to get too heated up,"

said Bennie seriously. "I'd better cool off with another drink."

Backwards and forwards went the fifty-cent piece. Down went the lemonade.

"We're doing the right thing, Ginge," said Bennie decisively. "Buying from each other and not just giving ourselves freebies."

"Too right, Bennie."

At last they reached the top of Welby Hill.

"Never thought we'd get here," said Ginger. "Let's set up."

He stared disbelievingly into the bucket. "Gosh!" he exclaimed. "It's . . . it's just about empty!"

"So it is, well . . . we may as well finish it," sighed Bennie.

Ginger nodded his agreement.

A quick swig each and the entire bucket of lemonade was gone. Wearily they slumped under the shade of the closest tree.

"Where did we go wrong?" said Bennie.

"Don't ask me," said Ginger. "You paid and I paid and still all we've got left is an empty bucket and a fifty-cent piece. There must be another way of running a business."

"Yeah, there must be," mumbled Bennie.

"It looks like another session with that monster Sargent, if I'm ever going to get that money to take Min to the show," said Ginger downheartedly. "C'mon, we might as well go home."

Chapter 10
Take Your Pick

WHEN Ginger and Bennie stumbled home after their disastrous efforts as purveyors of soft drink, they failed to notice a slyly grinning little face poke up from behind a bush in the park. Darky Nolan had quickly hidden there when he had sighted Ginger and Bennie struggling up the hill. He'd been close enough to hear all that went on. "I've got a feeling Coogan would like to know what you're up to Meggsie," he muttered to himself.

Darky found Coogan with Bobby Baxter throwing stones at the pigeons in Gawler's Paddock. Not their normal practice, but inexplicably there weren't many sparrows around.

"What do you want, Nolan?" scowled Coogan, seeing Darky approaching. "M' wheelbarrow's at home," he laughed sarcastically, and winked at Baxter, who also laughed and winked back.

"Something I thought you might want to know about

Meggsie," answered Darky, strangely flattened by Coogan's cynical greeting.

"Meggsie?" Coogan said, suddenly attentive. "What about him?"

"I just overheard him and Hooper in the park. It seems Meggsie's flat broke and is trying to raise some money."

"That all?" yawned Coogan. "Ginger Meggs is always trying to raise money. So what's new?"

"He has to get it by tomorrow, so he can take Minnie Peters to the gala show on Australia Day."

"So Meggsie wants money, eh? To go to the show, eh?"

Coogan was indeed interested. This was the chance he was looking for. At last he could have his just revenge.

"SO MEGGSIE WANTS TO GO TO THE SHOW, EH?"

"Listen, Nolan," he said menacingly, "do you want to do yourself a favour, by doing me a favour?"

Nolan was slightly confused by Coogan's turn of phrase, but nodded just the same.

"Wise move," said Coogan smartly. "Here's what we're going to do."

Ginger sat on his front fence desperately trying to think of some way to make the money he needed. Time was running out fast. It was the day before the parade and so far it had proved disastrous.

Not only hadn't he earned anything but he was still smarting from the money lost on the lemonade venture. Bennie had ended up with the sole fifty-cent piece while he had forked out eighty-four cents at the supermarket for the sugar.

That, Ginger calculated, made him five dollars thirty-four in arrears.

Mrs Sargent did want someone to look after Glennie late in the afternoon but even if he could bring himself to do it, the most he could hope for was two dollars. It didn't take a financial giant to work out that he still wouldn't have enough for two tickets. "And a feller would probably end up spending the night washing ink out of his hair," he thought to himself.

Just then, Herbie Haeburn and Normie had arrived at the Meggses' fence.

"Still teaching y' little brother the great lessons of life?" asked Ginger dryly.

"No, Meggsie," Herbie answered, "he knows them all

now. This week we're making money to go to the Australia Day show."

Ginger's eyes lit up.

"How's it going?" he enquired.

"Far out," said Herbie proudly, his thumbs tucked under the lapels of his jacket. "We are making big brass, and I do mean big."

"How big?"

"Would you believe seven dollars twenty-eight cents in only five days!"

Ginger was impressed, but at the same time puzzled: how could two fellers, not nearly as smart as he was at earning a living, be so successful?

"We got an act," explained Herbie proudly. "Well to be strictly correct, Normie here's the act, I'm the manager."

"WE GOT AN ACT."

Ginger looked at little Normie standing quietly below him.

"Looks like Herbie's had him jumping out of more trees," he thought.

"What exactly is the act?" asked Ginger.

That was opening enough for Herbie.

"I have a boy here who does great imitations. For twenty cents he will imitate a hen."

"Big deal," thought Ginger.

"What will he do?" he asked. "Cackle?"

"No, no, Ginger," boasted Herbie. "No cheap imitations from the Haeburn Brothers. No. For twenty cents he'll eat a worm."

Ginger's stomach did a somersault as he watched Herbie proudly lead Normie off down the street. Just then the thought of revolting Glennie Sargent wasn't too bad. He was trying not to think about worms — or ink — when Bobby Baxter's face popped around the corner of the fence.

"Hey, Meggsie," he said, "you tryin' to raise some money or something?"

"What's it to you, Baxter?" Ginger replied guardedly.

"Nothing, except this old feller down the road gave me fifty cents to give you this envelope. Said he'd heard you were down on y' luck," said Baxter.

"An old feller? What old feller?" asked Ginger.

"Don't know. He had a white beard and glasses and wore sandshoes. He just said to give you this."

Baxter handed Ginger the envelope. Ginger eyed it suspiciously.

"Well . . . aren't you going to open it?" said Baxter. "It might be money."

Ginger slowly tore the envelope apart. "It's an old bit of paper," he said, a little disappointed.

"Show us," said Baxter, virtually snatching it out of Ginger's hands.

"Not just a bit of old paper, mate," said Baxter excitedly, "it's a map — a treasure map. Boy, are you lucky!"

Ginger grabbed the map from Baxter and studied it intently.

"Sure looks like it," he said.

"Looks like your money problems are solved Meggsie," said Baxter.

"Treasure map?" muttered Ginger. "Where to?"

"HE FELL FOR IT, EDDIE."

He looked up but Baxter had gone.

"Well, I've got nothing to lose," he said, jumping off the fence. "Let's just look into this 'treasure map'. First it says to go to Dolan's stable door. That's not far from here. C'mon, fellers," he called to Mike and Tony and the three raced off at a great pace.

Not far away, huddled together behind a telephone pole, were Coogan, Baxter and Nolan.

"He fell for it, Eddie," sniggered Baxter.

"Yeah!" grinned Coogan, showing all his teeth.

Ginger arrived puffing at Dolan's stable. Propped up against the door was a pick with a note attached to the handle.

"This must be the place," said Ginger. "It's still all very strange, if you ask me."

Tony pulled the note from the pick and gave it to Ginger.

"Take this pick and go to Gawler's Paddock," the note instructed.

"Oh well, why not?" said Ginger. "I've come this far. The big brass is there, I bet."

At Gawler's Paddock Ginger found a second note. This time he had to walk eighty paces to the "Square Leg" tree stump, then turn right and proceed another twenty paces north. There would be more instructions there.

"Boy, that old bloke's been busy, I bet," Ginger said to Mike and Tony, and again the three set off as instructed.

"Eighteen, nineteen, twenty. That should do it," said Ginger as he paced off the final steps.

He looked around; at first there appeared to be nothing out of the ordinary. Then out of the corner of his eye he noticed the end of a bit of rag sticking out of the ground, flapping in the breeze.

Ginger bent down, pulled it up and brushed the dirt away. Something had been scribbled across the cloth: "This is it! Dig two feet down at this spot," it read.

Ginger began digging furiously. Mike and Tony helped push the dirt aside.

"There *IS* something there. You beaut!" exclaimed Ginger, as excited as he'd ever been.

He bent down and started scraping away the dirt with his hands.

"I've got whatever it is," he said, tugging at the unknown object. "One hard yank . . ."

Up it came with a shower of dirt.

"Oh no!" said Ginger, horrified at his discovery. "It's a DEAD CAT. Oh yuk!"

He dropped the smelly object back in the hole.

It was then that the pieces began to fit together and it dawned on him what had happened.

"This is Coogan's work, I bet," he said bitterly through clenched teeth.

Out of sight, on the far side of Gawler's Paddock in the long grass, Eddie Coogan watched satisfied that everything had gone as he'd planned. He grinned at Nolan and Baxter.

"You're not wrong, Meggs," he said under his breath, then turned to Nolan and Baxter.

"I'll see you guys later; there's something else important I have to do," he laughed.

Minnie and Coogan were chatting on the Peterses' front door step when much to Coogan's surprise a whistling and extremely happy-looking Ginger came sauntering up the garden path.

"Hello, Ginger," said Minnie.

"Ah, there, Min," said Ginger cheerily. "And how might *you* be, Mister Coogan?"

"I hear you've been digging, Mister Meggs," Coogan smirked. "Did you find the treasure?" he sneered. "Take your pick, did you?"

"THIS IS COOGAN'S WORK, I BET."

Ginger threw his arms around Coogan, which surprised Minnie almost as much as it surprised Coogan himself.

"No," said Ginger, "I didn't take *my* pick, but I sold the one I found for fifteen dollars," and he casually pulled the money out of his pocket for all to see.

Coogan was thunderstruck.

"Now, if you'll pardon me, Mister Coogan," Ginger continued as he elbowed Coogan aside, "I have something to ask Miss Peters."

He gruffly pushed Coogan aside.

"I was wondering, Min, if you'd like to come with me to the Australia Day parade and to the show after. It'll be real t'rific, I bet."

Minnie remained silent and gently bit her lip.

"She can't," interrupted Coogan smugly. "She's already going with me. Aren't you, Min?"

Ginger and Coogan both looked at Minnie. After what seemed an eternity she spoke. "I guess so," she said quietly.

"Great!" shouted Coogan. "I'll pick you up tomorrow arvo. Dad's got beaut seats for us, right in the front row."

Now it was Ginger's turn to be elbowed aside and Coogan strutted, like a peacock, off home.

Ginger tried to speak but the words stuck in his throat.

"I'm sorry, Ginger, really sorry. I wanted you to ask me, but I didn't think you would. I waited, I really did," said Minnie sincerely.

"That's okay, Min." Ginger was dashed but tried hard

139

to put on a brave face. "You'll have a top time, I know. I'll be seeing you round, I guess."

Minnie watched sadly as Ginger drooped down the path, with Mike and Tony at his heels.

Chapter 11
Just the Chance of a Lifetime

IT was Australia Day, the day of the big parade and gala show.

Ginger sat mournfully at his favourite corner. He hadn't been this depressed since the day England had beaten Australia in the third test after the Aussies had enforced the "follow on".

"Ah, what's the use?" he thought. "A feller might just as well head off round the world as stay in this place. He'd be better off in China or America or one of those big towns."

Mike licked Ginger's hand sympathetically.

"Don't worry, feller. I'll take you with me, for sure."

Tony jumped onto Ginger's shoulder.

"I'd take both of you," he said, forcing a smile.

Bennie and Chubb, their hands in their pockets and their faces almost as glum as Ginger's, strolled up and plomped down next to him. For a while nothing was said, then Chubb spoke: "It's a bit rough, eh, Ginge?"

"You heard, then?" replied Ginger.

"Everyone's heard," said Bennie in a near whisper. "That viper Coogan hasn't wasted any time telling the world he's taking Min to the Australia Day parade and gala show."

"And what a fool he made of you," added Chubb. "He had all the weeds down at Joe's in stitches."

"Did you really dig up a dead cat?" asked Bennie. "That's what Nolan reckons."

Ginger looked glumly at Bennie and nodded slowly.

"Gee, Coogan will drive me crazy bragging for the next year, I bet," he said, almost becoming angry. "A feller's got a good mind to turn up anyway and just stare at the creep to make him feel uncomfortable."

"That's just what he'd want you to do, I bet," said Chubb knowingly.

"You're probably right," said Ginger. "Min would think I was a dag for doing that, anyway. A guy just can't win."

The more Ginger thought about it the more depressed he became. There was just no way out of it. No way at all...or was there?

Slowly his eyes opened wide and began to sparkle, a grin began to grow between his freckles. He started muttering wildly to himself.

"Of course a guy can win," he shouted, leaping to his feet. "Of course he can!"

Mike and Tony jumped back, startled.

"He can?" questioned Bennie, confused.

"How?" asked Chubb, just as confused.

"I'm not going *to* the parade or *to* the show, I'm going

142

to be *in* the parade and *in* the show," he said confidently. "That'll fix Coogan once and for all."

"Unreal!" said Chubb. "Ripper!"

"It *sounds* like a fantabulous idea," said Bennie, deeply concerned.

"Do y' reckon they'll let you in?" asked Chubb.

"Why not?" said Ginger. "The sign said residents of the district can participate, and I'm one of them."

"If you went as something really Australian, Ginger, I reckon they'd have to let you in," advised Chubb.

"Like a bushranger," suggested Bennie eagerly. "Go as Ned Kelly!"

"Hey, yeah!" said Ginger, nimbly working out his assets for the role. "Ned Kelly! I've got a big old ice-cream tin I could wear as a helmet, and I could carry that busted old gun of Dad's; it'd look t'rific."

"And you could use Riley's goat as a horse," said Chubb.

"Yeah," said Ginger. "We'd better hurry but; it's only a couple of hours till the parade starts."

"I'll get Riley's goat for you, Ginge," said Chubb, already running down the street. "See y' at your house."

"Good one, Chubb," Ginger shouted, "but be quiet, it's got to be a terrible great secret between us!"

He smiled broadly at Bennie. "Wait till Coogan sees me!" he crowed.

"Don't you dare move until I get a picture of this," said Mrs Meggs, hurrying into the house and in her excitement slamming the wire door behind her.

"Watch the door," winced Mr Meggs. "Women!" he added. The door had banged just as loudly as if it was Ginger passing through, but he, at that moment, was sitting in the middle of the yard, a truly resplendent figure on Riley's goat, helmet gleaming, gun holstered — Ned Kelly without a doubt.

In only an hour, Ginger, with the help of Bennie and Chubb, had been transformed into a small sized version of the notorious Victorian outlaw.

Bennie had borrowed his brother's science room dustcoat. It fitted Ginger perfectly — once the sleeves were rolled up and the hem had been pinned back a centimetre or five.

Chubb had saddled Riley's goat with his baby sister's bunny rug. His mum didn't know about that yet, but he was sure she'd have said yes if he'd asked, so he grabbed it out of his sister's cot anyway.

Even Mr Meggs had helped out by carefully cutting a neat slot in the ice-cream tin so that Ginger could see where he was going, and hadn't objected when Ginger had asked to borrow the old, broken revolver.

The back wire door slammed again. Mr Meggs raised one eyebrow and frowned at his wife.

"Oh, I'm sorry, John," said Mrs Meggs, "but this is just so exciting. Imagine our son in a parade with the Prime Minister himself. Okay, Ginger, smile!" she said, holding up her camera.

"Don't be silly, Sarah," grumbled Mr Meggs. "You won't know if he's smiling or not. You can't see his mouth, only his eyes."

"Well, I'll know. Now say 'cheese'."

"Gee, Mum," Ginger's voice echoed deeply from inside his helmet, "Ned Kelly would never say cheese. He'd say, 'Stick 'em up or I'll shoot to kill'."

"Say whatever you like, Ginger. But say *something*," said Mrs Meggs.

"Stick 'em up or I'll shoot to kill!" said Ginger, as seriously as he could, in his deepest possible voice, and waving the gun around.

"Gosh, Ginge, you look exactly like the real thing!" exclaimed Bennie.

"Snap!" The camera clicked!

"You'd better hurry down to the Town Hall, Ned," smiled Mr Meggs proudly. "Takes after his father, that boy."

"STICK 'EM UP OR I'LL SHOOT TO KILL!"

"As a Meggs or a Kelly?" asked Mrs Meggs mischievously.

Ginger proudly cantered Riley's goat down to the Town Hall with Tony perched behind him and Mike capering at their feet. He made sure he used as many back lanes as he could. It was no use showing off just yet and taking the risk of being spotted by one of Coogan's clan, or even by Coogan himself.

The element of surprise was of the utmost importance if Ginger was to emerge triumphant over his old time rival.

"You stay here, feller," said Ginger, carefully tying up Riley's goat to one of the tastefully sculptured Egyptian lions in front of the Town Hall. "I won't be long." He put his helmet under one arm and walked up the steps. Tony and Mike were not prepared to miss anything and followed at their master's heels.

Inside the Town Hall it was almost as gloomy as the public library and a lot colder. Instead of marble statues the walls were covered in paintings of old men in funny-looking clothes.

At first glance it seemed deserted.

"I hope they haven't all gone to the parade," whispered a concerned Ginger to Tony.

"Lost, are you, sonny?" asked someone from behind.

"Oh!" said Ginger, startled, and turned to see where the voice came from.

Sitting quietly on a wooden pew in the waiting area of the Council Chambers was a tall, elderly gentleman. He was suntanned and bearded and dressed in western gear, ten-gallon hat and all.

"No, mister," said Ginger. "I'm just looking for the guy who's organising the parade this arvo."

"That'd be Councillor Jenvey," said the cowboy-looking character, indicating the office opposite him.

Ginger moved towards the closed door.

"I think he's got someone in there with him at the moment. You can join the queue if you want."

"Queue?" enquired Ginger.

"Me; the name's Dusty," he said. "Howdy."

"G'day, I'm Ginger Meggs."

They shook hands.

"And you're going to be in the parade are you, Ginger?" asked Dusty.

"I reckon; and are you?"

"No, but I am in the show afterwards. And what might you be?"

Ginger quickly slipped his helmet over his head.

"Ned Kelly," he said gruffly.

"Well, well, well, Ginger, me old partner," laughed Dusty loudly. "You'd better keep away from me, seeing as I'm driving the old Cobb and Co. stage coach. Ned was rather fond of them in the old days, you know."

"Wow!" said Ginger, impressed. He removed his helmet and added. "Unreal!"

The office door opened and Councillor Jenvey emerged, shaking hands with someone dressed like Captain Cook.

"Right, who was next?" he said lightly. "Ah, Dusty, what can I do for you?"

"It's okay, I can wait, Stewart," said Dusty. "I believe this young bloke here wanted to see you."

He indicated to Ginger, who smiled broadly.

"Ginger Meggs, meet Councillor Jenvey. Councillor Jenvey, this is Ginger Meggs."

"What can I do for you, Ginger?" asked the Councillor politely.

"I'd like to go in the parade and the show, sir, as Ned Kelly. I've got my goat outside and everything," said Ginger enthusiastically.

Councillor Jenvey grimaced and shook his head, "I'm sorry, Ginger, but you can't go into the procession or the show, I'm afraid. All the arrangements are already made."

Ginger was floored. His world had crashed about him for the second time in as many days.

"But," he pleaded, "I borrowed Riley's goat and... and Bennie's brother's coat." A tear began to swell up in his eye, "And I'm one of those residents of the district like it said on the sign and all."

"There's nothing I can do, I'm afraid, Ginger," said Councillor Jenvey, sincerely. "You're a day late. Applications closed yesterday."

Ginger could see there was no use pleading any further with the Councillor. He looked at Dusty, who shrugged sympathetically.

Ginger trudged lifelessly towards the front door,

149

"THERE'S NOTHING I CAN DO, GINGER."

Councillor Jenvey's words ringing in his ears. "Closed yesterday, closed yesterday, closed yesterday." It was too much. The tears began running down his face.

Ginger wiped his face with his sleeve and walked out into the sunlight. He sat on the Town Hall steps and looked wistfully at Mike and Tony.

"Gee, y'd think they'd let a feller in," he said.

Ginger was still sitting on the steps when Dusty came out of the Town Hall.

"I'm sorry you weren't able to go in the parade, Ginger," he said. "A real bit of bad luck, that."

"Ah, it doesn't matter, Dusty," replied Ginger, now over the worst of his disappointment. "There'll be other parades, I bet."

"You bet there will, matey," said Dusty.

Ginger watched as the genial old cowboy walked off up the street. He had only gone a couple of metres when, without any warning, a huge, unshaven, ugly-looking man slid out of the shadows behind him. Ginger could see he was holding a gun at Dusty's head.

It took a second to register — Dusty was being held up.

"Okay, cocky," said the robber. "Freeze, or I'll blow y' back to the country."

Dusty did as he was told.

"I know you blokes are always loaded. Come on, hand over your dough, and make it quick."

Ginger knew he had to do *something*. But what? Top footballer that he was he couldn't tackle someone that big. It could be fatal but there wasn't time to run for help.

He had an idea, not much of an idea, but it was better than nothing. He picked up his father's broken old gun from the steps, crossed his fingers, then crept towards Dusty and his assailant.

"Hurry up, hurry up, I haven't got all day," snarled the robber, becoming more menacing.

Dusty fished in his pockets for his wallet.

By now Ginger was right behind them. He breathed deeply, stood on the tips of his toes, then in as deep a voice as possible said, "Stick 'em up, or I'll shoot to kill."

With that he poked the old revolver into the scoundrel's back.

The robber immediately dropped his gun and threw his hands in the air. Dusty quickly seized the weapon.

"STICK 'EM UP, OR I'LL SHOOT TO KILL."

"Good on y', Ginger," he said. "Your bluff worked, but it took some nerve to do it."

"Huh?" exclaimed the robber. Turning around and seeing Ginger standing below him with the broken gun, he added, "You've got to be joking."

Dusty waved the gun in his face. "This is no joke and that's enough from you," he said. "But Ginger, you've given me an idea. Let's hand this ornery critter over to the police and I'll tell you all about it."

Everyone who was anyone hustled into the Town Hall auditorium that evening. There was much copious back-slapping and hand-shaking amongst the organising officials. It seemed everyone agreed what a huge success the Australia Day parade had been and if the gala show was anywhere near half as good, it would be a treat indeed.

The festival atmosphere was carried into the auditorium itself, as most of the characters from the procession had remained in costume and added gay colour to the otherwise drab hall.

Eddie Coogan jostled his way down the aisle, as the house lights began to fade. Minnie was a couple of metres behind, doing her best to keep up.

"Hurry up, Min," shouted Coogan, over the din, "you'll miss the opening."

The National Anthem began just as Min reached her seat. She looked icily at Coogan.

"The least you could have done was wait," she said.

Before Coogan could answer, the National Anthem had reached a crescendo and drowned out his feeble excuse.

Then the Mayor coughed into the microphone and tapped it a couple of times.

"Honoured guests," he began, "ladies and gentlemen, citizens of this great country, I thank you for coming along here today and making it the great success that it has been. Not since..."

The Mayor continued at great length, but nobody appeared to mind.

"I bet Meggsie wishes he was here," whispered Coogan.

"Shush!" whispered Minnie.

"...and now, without further ado, let me proudly

153

introduce to you the Prime Minister of this great country."

The hall erupted with applause, whistling, cheering and foot stamping as the Prime Minister entered. He raised his hands and quietened the crowd.

"Ladies and gentlemen, boys and girls, and even little babies, yes, fellow Australians, on this our National Day, let me say unequivocally how happy I am to be here..."

There was more rapturous applause.

"Having said that, let me say this..." he continued.

The audience was transfixed by his every word; they sat glued to the edge of their seats.

"...and finally, it's my pleasure, and indeed my honour, to introduce the first act on the programme, Mr Dusty Wheels, and another Australian folk legend, in a scene from our not-too-distant past."

The enormous crowd applauded as the Prime Minister left the stage and the curtains opened, revealing Dusty and his Cobb and Co. coach and team of horses.

"Unreal! Ex-cell-ent!" shouted Coogan.

Dusty began his act by singing a country version of "I Still Call Australia Home", at the end of which he bowed and gracefully acknowledged the applauding crowd. He then pretended to bring the horses to a standstill.

"Whoa up, boys, looks like trouble ahead," he said, looking into the wings. "Why it looks like that young bushranger, Kelly the Kid."

That was the cue. Now was the big moment.

On to centre stage rode a helmeted Ginger on Riley's goat, brandishing an old revolver.

The audience laughed and cheered.

"Go for it, son," screamed Coogan, not knowing who was beneath the tin mask.

"Stick 'em up or I'll shoot to kill," said Ginger loudly.

Dusty went for his shotgun. A shot rang out and the gun went spinning from his hand.

Ginger blew down the barrel of his revolver. Spontaneous cheering broke out in the auditorium.

"Wow! What a tough kid! He's tops, isn't he, Min?" said Coogan. "He'd take Meggs apart, I bet."

Minnie ignored his comments.

"Let that be a warning to you. Now throw over your money and I'll be going," said Ginger.

Dusty threw down a large satchel. Ginger opened it and threw a handful of paper money back into the coach.

"Never let it be said that Kelly the Kid wasn't fair," he said, galloping off into the wings.

"And so began the career of Edward 'Ned' Kelly," said a voice over the loudspeaker system.

The audience cheered wildly.

"More! More!" they shouted. "Bring back Kelly the Kid."

Dusty got down from the coach and walked to the front of the stage.

A hush fell over the audience.

"Mr Prime Minister, Mr Mayor, honoured guests, fellow Aussies. What you have just seen is a little play the young feller and I worked out for your amusement. He doesn't know I'm going to do this," said Dusty, grinning. "Hey, Kelly, get out here."

Ginger ran back on stage.

"You've just seen how a young bloke held me up." Dusty bent down and put his arms around Ginger's shoulders. "Well, this arvo, it was quite the opposite. This young feller here stopped me from being robbed — single-handed. I go so far as to say he saved m' bloomin' life. It was just the chance of a lifetime he happened along when he did."

He gave Ginger an appreciative squeeze and took an envelope from his pocket.

"It's not much, but I got a little reward for him. A brand new one hundred dollar note."

"Wow!" echoed out of the tin helmet as Ginger sighted the money.

Dusty stood up.

"And now, Mr Prime Minister, ladies and gentlemen, please stand and join me in a rousing round of applause to one of the coolest characters and bravest little blokes you could meet — your own..."

Dusty lifted the helmet off Ginger's head.

"...Ginger Meggs! All together now...

Hip hip — hooray!
Hip hip — hooray!
Hip hip — hooray!"

The cheering was even louder than it had been for the Prime Minister's entrance. The Town Hall seemed to shake under the thunderous noise.

Coogan stood open-mouthed, refusing to believe what he was seeing or hearing. Next to him stood Minnie, beaming from ear to ear.

"HIP HIP HOORAY !!"

"And to think I stood up and cheered 'MORE!'," muttered Coogan.

The applause seemed to go on for ages.

All Ginger could do was stand modestly in the middle of the stage, his tousled red hair hanging over his forehead, his eyes downcast.

He glanced up for a moment, in time to see Minnie wave frantically and blow him a kiss.

"I bet I'm the luckiest feller in Australia," he thought.

No one could argue with that!

Dear Reader,

Have you ever stopped to think about the pictures on stamps and the stories behind them?

Australia Post has issued a set of stamps about Classic Children's Books. This is just one example of the stories stamps can tell. And this, of course, adds lots of interest and enjoyment to stamp collecting — which is a great hobby to start with!

Having read this book on Ginger Meggs you'll have some idea of just how much there is to say about the Ginger Meggs stamp. And it's the same with all stamps — every one of them has a story behind it which you could find out about.

If you'd like to find out about the new stamps coming out, Australia Post has two booklets they'd be happy to send to you, free of charge. Both booklets come out up to six times each year.

So if you'd like to start collecting stamps (and stories) and are under 12, you can receive the Junior Stamp Preview. All you need do is write to the following address giving your full name, address and most importantly, date of birth:

Junior Stamp Preview
PO Box 511
SOUTH MELBOURNE VIC 3205

If you're over 12, the Australian Stamp Bulletin is for you — and you can get it by sending your name and address to:

Australian Stamp Bulletin
Locked Bag 8
SOUTH MELBOURNE VIC 3205

(if you're under 18, please add your date of birth).

ANGUS & ROBERTSON PUBLISHERS

Unit 4, Eden Park, 31 Waterloo Road,
North Ryde, NSW, Australia 2113, and
16 Golden Square, London W1R 4BN,
United Kingdom

First published in Australia
by Angus & Robertson Publishers in 1985
First published in the United Kingdom
by Angus & Robertson (UK) Ltd in 1985

Copyright © James Kemsley and
Jimera Pty Ltd 1985

National Library of Australia
Cataloguing-in-publication data.

Kemsley, James, 1948- .
    Ginger Meggs at large.

    ISBN 0 207 15194 6.

    1. Children's stories, Australian.
    I. Bancks, J. C. (James Charles), 1889-1952.
    II. Title.
A823'.3

Typeset in 12 pt Baskerville by The Type Shop
Printed in Australia by The Dominion Press–Hedges & Bell